GONE

DARK

CJ LYONS

Also By CJ Lyons:

Lucy Guardino Thrillers:
SNAKE SKIN
BLOOD STAINED
KILL ZONE
AFTER SHOCK
HARD FALL
BAD BREAK
LAST LIGHT
OPEN GRAVE

Hart and Drake Medical Suspense:
NERVES OF STEEL
SLEIGHT OF HAND
FACE TO FACE
EYE OF THE STORM

Shadow Ops Covert Thrillers:
CHASING SHADOWS
LOST IN SHADOWS
EDGE OF SHADOWS

Fatal Insomnia Medical Thrillers:
FAREWELL TO DREAMS
A RAGING DAWN
THE SLEEPLESS STARS

This book is a work of fiction. Any references to historical events, real people, or real locales are used fictitiously. Other names, characters, places, and incidents are the product of the author's imagination, and any resemblance to actual events or locales or persons, living or dead, is entirely coincidental and not intended by the author.

GONE

DARK

CJ LYONS

Chapter 1

October 17, 2006
Craven County, TN

Between the weight of Hank's body and his blood slicked over my eyes, nose, and mouth, I couldn't breathe. Actually, I didn't care about breathing. What I really wanted to do was scream.

I opened my mouth, and the stench of blood mixed with gunpowder made me retch. I locked my jaws, teeth grinding, to hold back soured orange juice vomit. Swallowing burnt my throat but helped me ignore the blood.

My elbows ground against the rough concrete floor as I heaved Hank off me. I heard a moan—not from him—and dropped the gun. It clattered against the floor, sliding under a coffee table strewn with playing cards, cigarette butts, a glass bong shaped like a dragon, red plastic cups, and the vodka bottle, all now speckled red with blood.

Music swelled, competing with the storm outside as it pounded against the cinderblock walls. Led Zeppelin, Jack had told me. Something about a hangman. Definitely not the kind of music we listened to at my gran's house—she was partial to Merle Haggard and George Strait. The thought of Gran, of what she would think had happened here tonight, of telling her...it was unbearable. I closed my eyes, took another breath, forcing myself not to gag, and opened them once more. *Please, God, let Jack be okay.*

I couldn't make it farther than my knees, not without my vision going swimmy and dark. I crawled the few feet to where Jack lay. It was obvious his one eye was gone—a cavernous black-rimmed hole brimming with blood was all that was left. But he wasn't dead. Not yet, anyway. His hand flapped toward me, landing in my lap like it had earlier in the night, but this time I didn't slap him away. This time I grabbed him and held on tight.

"It'll be okay," I kept saying. I knew I should say something else, comfort him, make everything right—as if words could ever fix what had happened here tonight—but my brain was sticky with cobwebs and I couldn't think of anything else to say. "It'll be okay."

"Hank," he mumbled. "Where's—"

I swiveled my body to block any chance of him seeing his twin brother; or what was left of him. Hank's face was pretty much gone, but worse was what was oozing out the back of his head. Despite the miserly light provided by a few bare bulbs swinging from the rafters, I could still see way too much. My stomach heaved and kicked, but Jack clutched my hand so tight all I could do was turn my head away, close my eyes against the sight of Hank's faceless body, and vomit in the direction of the floor drain. From the burn, I guessed maybe there'd been vodka in the OJ—I knew there'd been something, the way my brain felt lighter than air and my lips were numb and I couldn't think through the cotton candy fuzz filling my head.

The twins had promised it was only orange juice, promised I didn't have to do anything I didn't want, promised I could stop anytime and they'd take me home... They'd lied.

But that didn't mean they deserved to die.

"Cherry," Jack called to me as if I weren't mere inches from him, "I can't see."

"Hang on." I wiped my mouth with the back of my hand.

I needed to call for help. I glanced around the small office—the twins had taken it over as a sort of clubhouse, but there was no phone that I could see. It wasn't even a proper office, just a corrugated tin roof over four concrete block walls set on a cement slab with a drain in the center—that drain now slick with undigested pretzels and clumps of OJ and mucus, but I couldn't help but wonder what that drain was there for, given that the massive barn the room connected to had once been a slaughterhouse. That's what the Kutlers were known for—beef. The best in Craven County, enough to feed hordes of hungry copper and coal miners, iron workers, truck drivers, and railroad men.

Of course, now all the mines and forges are closed, and with them the trucks and trains have gone as well. Along with the cows. The Kutlers still own the land, now used for four-wheeling and paintball wars. Somehow, despite the rest of the county losing just about everything, they still managed to thrive. Not by much, but so far ahead of the rest of us that everyone ducked their head in a nod of respect when the Kutlers passed by.

All night long Jack kept making the joke, over and over, until even Hank stopped laughing at it. *C'mon, Cherrygirl, let me show you my beef.*

As the words flew through my head, I gagged. Tried to throw up some more, but all that came out was bile. My body heaved, Jack's moans punctuating my coughing. Help; I needed to get help.

The cheap door rattled and the tin roof pinged, the storm outside still lashing wind and rain against the building. There were no windows, and I had no idea what time it was—time seemed muddled, filled with gaps I couldn't connect.

I remembered school, riding my bike home when the storm hit, pumping my legs as hard as I could up the steep switchbacks; then the roar of the truck, my scream when it almost hit me, skidding through the mud and gravel and into the kudzu and scrub oaks lining the side of the road. Hank tossing my bike into the back of the pickup like it weighed nothing, me climbing into the front seat between him and Jack, their legs pressed against mine, both so warm. Hank shoving Jack away from me as he wrapped his arm around my shoulders and squeezed, told me everything was going to be okay, my bike wasn't hurt that bad and he could fix anything, I'd see...

Gran had bought me that bike last Christmas, used at the St. Vincent's, but she'd painted it, made it look all shiny and new again. She'd kill me if anything happened to it. *Gran—where's Gran? Right. In the hospital.* Part of the reason I'd ended up here to start with. *She's gonna be so mad at me.* I didn't want to, but I couldn't help but glance at Hank's body. *Everyone will be. Think, Cherish, think. Help. Call 911.*

One of the twins—it took me a moment to remember which one—had slid my phone out of my coat pocket the first time I'd asked to leave. Jack; it had been Jack, I was almost sure, my memories of just a few hours ago already faded and worn as thin as the frayed holes in my jeans. I was only fourteen, had never been drunk before—I guess I'd thought throwing up would help clear out the alcohol or something, but it was still hard to think straight. *Phone. Right. I need a phone.* Even if not mine—well, Gran's, really. She'd bought it so they could call her into work when they needed extra help at the chicken plant over in Cleveland. Before she got sick.

Phone. Jack had one. Both twins did—those fancy, slimmer, shiny ones that did so much more than just make calls. Gingerly, I patted his pockets, sliding one hand beneath his butt—something that normally would have thrown me into a panic attack. Me, Cherish Walker, trailer-trash freshman nobody, daring to touch the great and mighty senior all-star wide receiver Jack Kutler's butt? Probably the most coveted ass in all of Craven County. Well, tied with his identical twin quarterback brother Hank's, that was.

Now, of course, none of that mattered, but I couldn't stop the thought, and thinking it had me giggling in a weird half scream, half crying way. I felt a hard slab of plastic and slid it free from his pocket. The screen blinked to life, and I dialed.

"911. What's your emergency?"

"Someone's been shot. The old Kutler slaughterhouse."

"What's your name, sweetheart?"

"Cherish Walker. Please hurry." I turned my head away from Jack, facing the puddle of my expelled stomach contents and Hank's lifeless body, and whispered, "I think he might be dying."

Chapter 2

Eleven years later...

Lucy Guardino steered her Subaru over the steeply curved country road south of Pittsburgh, the car's headlights carving a white blare through the pitch black. She should slow down—hitting a deer at this speed would be a death sentence. But the churning anxiety tugging at her stomach wouldn't let her.

"Are you there yet?" her husband's disembodied voice asked via the car's speakers. Nick was at a traumatologist conference in Orlando, leaving Lucy alone to deal with...well, whatever the hell this was. Probably nothing; hopefully nothing.

"No." Her tone was clipped, and she

worked to soften it. It wasn't Nick's fault. "Almost."

"I keep trying their landline but no answer. Should I call the police?" His voice tightened with fear.

"It's unincorporated county land. This time of night, any calls would go to the Staties. I'm closer." She jerked the wheel and hit the brakes. There was a narrow lane up ahead—or was it just a gap in the trees? No, it was definitely a road—not paved, gravel. She glanced at her nav screen. All it showed was a mass of green. Then her headlights caught the glint of a mailbox.

"I found it." She turned down the drive. The first quarter mile she couldn't see anything through the thick forest, but then the trees gave way to reveal a wide lawn and buildings. A large barn and a few smaller outbuildings along with two houses—one a traditional farm house that looked like it could have been there for a century or more, the other a sprawling modern ranch all glass and sharp angles.

An assortment of vehicles was parked on

the drive and grass, clustered in front of the newer house. Music pulsated through the sweltering July night.

As Lucy pulled up and parked, she spotted several couples in various states of undress making out in the cars. She grabbed her phone, switched the call over, and exited the Subaru.

Her hand went to her hip, where her Beretta 9mm was holstered on the waistband of her jeans, checking that it was still secure. Despite the fact that she'd left the FBI earlier in the year, after fifteen years with the Bureau, old habits wouldn't die—especially not with her daughter involved. She tugged the hem of her faded Penguins tee back over the semi-automatic; almost thought twice about carrying the weapon into a house filled with drunk, partying teenagers. But her daughter was somewhere inside—along with who-knew-what.

Megan's smart and strong. She can take care of herself. Lucy tried to soothe the anxiety and paranoia tap-dancing up and down her every nerve ending. She'd faced serial killers with less fear.

"I'm sure she's fine." Nick's voice came from her cell phone, barely carrying over the music and the sounds of laughter and shouting coming from behind the house. "Remember to give her a chance."

A chance? Megan was fifteen; coming to this party—which was supposed to have been supervised by adults—*was* her chance. As far as Lucy was concerned, she'd failed it. Missed curfew, hadn't called, didn't answer when Lucy tried to text and call her, and clearly Megan had misjudged her so-called friends. And where were the parents? Lucy had phoned the mother yesterday; she'd promised everything was under control. *Just a summer pool party. Burgers on the grill, games of Marco Polo, some music and dancing. Nothing to worry about. I'll be here the whole time.*

Two girls stumbled out of the house, giggling even as one spun away to vomit into the shrubbery lining the walkway.

Right. Nothing to worry about.

"I think she's out of chances," Lucy muttered as she hung up. The second girl tried to help her friend by holding her hair out of her face, but instead fell, knocking them both into the hydrangeas and the puddle of vomit. They squealed and laughed, not even noticing Lucy.

She strode up the path and through the open front doors. The house had a quasi-Frank Lloyd Wright style to it, with angled high ceilings and exposed beams framing large windows and an open floor plan. From the foyer she could see all the way into the rear of the house where the kitchen stood, and more large windows and sliding doors leading out to a pool and patio. The pool's underwater lights were on, casting weird blue shadows on the figures cavorting in the water.

The lights were off in the front room and all of the furniture was shoved back, creating an impromptu dance floor filled with girls gyrating to the harsh, throbbing noises and misogynistic lyrics that passed for music nowadays. The boom of the bass line vibrated through the floorboards, up through Lucy's sneakers. She'd left the house so fast she hadn't stopped to put her ankle brace on and was already regretting the loss of its comforting stability.

Couples along with lone boys sprawled on the furniture, watching the dancers or engrossed with each other. The smell of marijuana and cigarettes clouded the air, mixing with aftershave, beer, and pheromones. Lucy used her phone as a flashlight, scanning the crowd, drawing scattered curses. Megan wasn't there.

As she moved through the throng of dancers, one of the girls grabbed her and tried to get Lucy to join her, her eyes glazed over, practically whimpering when Lucy detached herself from the dancer's embrace. More than marijuana and alcohol, Lucy diagnosed. MDMA or one of its many variations? *Damn*. She knew she should never have let Megan come tonight, even though she was certain Megan would never use drugs herself, and she'd long ago given her the roofie talk along with a detection stick that looked just like a regular coffee stirrer.

Megan was smart. But she was also fifteen. For the first time, Lucy regretted having let the school advance her a grade when they moved to

Pittsburgh from Virginia. Looking around at the scowls and leers from the almost-men draped over the furniture or standing against the wall, stalking the dancers' movements with predatory gazes, she realized that even though these other kids were only a year or two older than Megan, it was a huge difference. Especially the boys. They radiated such arrogance, confidence—how many times had Lucy faced those exact same expressions across from her in an interrogation room?

Don't be paranoid, she heard Nick's voice in her head. *Just because your life is filled with the one percent of humanity's dregs, don't pre-judge the rest of us.* She tried to look at the boys through Nick's psychologist's eyes. He was so much more forgiving and understanding than she was. But then one of the guys pushed off the wall and intertwined his arms around the dancing girl who'd tried to stop Lucy. He effortlessly separated her from the crowd, ending with her pinned against the wall, his gaze challenging Lucy as he ran his tongue along the girl's bare throat and slid his hand up under her shirt.

Lucy stopped, almost diverted from her mission, but no. Megan first. Then she'd deal with the rest. But she did inch her T-shirt up, exposing the nine-millimeter, flashing the kid a grin as she took a photo of him with her phone. He backed away from the girl, hiding his face.

She crossed into the kitchen. The lights were on here, revealing a chaos of plastic cups, spilled beverages smearing the floor with a slick and sticky coating, and various snacks scattered over every surface. A couple was making out against the refrigerator, and from the laundry room behind them another couple's shadows danced along the walls. She took a few steps to make sure Megan wasn't there, then went through the open sliding doors to the brick patio and the pool.

Out here the music shuffled from reggae to Beach Boys to hip-hop. A few kids splashed in the pool, couples filled the hot tub, a quintet of boys surrounded the keg urging one another to chug, and more couples occupied every chair and lounger. The backyard stretched out to the forest in the distance. Some partyers had spread out blankets, their forms barely visible in the moonlight.

Her anxiety worsening with every step, Lucy wove her way through the labyrinth of teens, searching for but not finding Megan. She received more than a few curses and threats as she interrupted several couples, always asking the girls if they were okay with what was happening, trying to assess their sobriety and ability to give consent while reminding herself that she was no longer law enforcement, merely a concerned civilian parent. The girls all seemed sober enough to consent—several proved that with extremely imaginative if anatomically incorrect vocabulary.

No one knew where Megan was. The closest Lucy got was a muttered "I think she's with Emma." Reassuring, since Emma was Megan's friend; not so reassuring as Emma was the one who'd invited Megan to the party. Emma was sixteen, with red curls and freckles that used to make her look younger than Megan—at least until last year, when she'd begun to develop and now had the figure of a twenty-something compared to Megan's relatively flat-chested, athletic build.

There was a small toolshed at the far end of the pool. Lucy flashed her light into the windows; only pool equipment. But she heard voices out back, low and urgent. One of them Megan's.

"I told you, we're leaving," Megan was saying as Lucy rounded the corner, coming up behind her.

Megan had one arm wrapped around Emma's waist, while Emma swayed and braced herself against the shed, her head drooping as if it were too much work to keep it upright. Facing them was a boy of maybe seventeen, wearing only swim shorts and a lecherous grin.

"How you gonna do that?" He sidled closer to Emma. "Emma doesn't want to go, do you, baby?"

Emma nodded, almost tipping her entire body into the boy's chest. Megan yanked her back. "Leave her alone."

Lucy stepped forward, the boy's eyes

widening as he spotted her. His expression morphed, but it was difficult to read in the dark. He swung his shoulders back, thrusting out his chest, muscles rippling, chin up, making it clear as he slunk back into the shadows that it wasn't defeat or surrender but a strategic retreat.

As if Lucy gave a shit. "Megan, Emma. We're going. Now." A high-octane mix of anger, anxiety, and adrenaline sent her words cracking through the night like gunshots.

Megan whirled. "Mom? What are you doing here?"

"Taking you home." Lucy moved to support Emma's other side. Both girls reeked of rum. Megan wore a T-shirt over her bathing suit, but it was sopping wet, clinging to her. Emma wore only her rather skimpy bikini. Neither girl had shoes on, slowing their progress, but Lucy had other concerns to distract her.

"I tried to call, but I lost my phone," Megan started, as they guided Emma across the lawn and around to the front of the house. Lucy winced at the way her words slurred.

"You're drunk. We'll talk about this tomorrow." They reached the Subaru. "If you're going to be sick, do it now while I call the police."

"The police?" Megan protested, as Emma slumped to her haunches, dry-heaving. "Mom. You can't. They'll blame me. Everyone will hate me."

"Help your friend." Lucy pivoted away and dialed.

Emma began vomiting and Megan quickly followed, a rancid puddle of rum and food sluicing from the grass onto the gravel. At least it wasn't inside the car, Lucy thought. As soon as she hung up from the police, she dialed Nick.

"She's safe." She started with the good news. "Drunk as a skunk, lost her phone, puking her guts out, and grounded for the rest of her natural-born days, but safe."

Chapter 3

"THIS IS CHILD ABUSE," Megan declared as they drove to Beacon Falls the next morning. She was wearing sunglasses and a woeful expression despite the aspirin and fluids Lucy had insisted upon. "Couldn't I just be grounded alone at home? In bed?"

"Except you wouldn't be alone. You'd be with the TV and Internet and your phone—no, wait, I forgot, your phone is at the bottom of a pool." That much she'd gotten out of Megan before Megan fell asleep last night. Lucy had stayed up all night watching her, remembering a college roommate who'd almost aspirated when she'd vomited in her sleep. Two decades later, the smell of Southern Comfort still made Lucy gag. "You're coming to work with me. Think of it as an unpaid internship."

Nick would be home tomorrow night. Together they'd decide how to handle the remainder of Megan's punishment. She was usually such an easy kid to handle—once she'd gotten past that awful pre-teen hormonal sniping and whining phase—that Lucy was at a loss now, torn between anger that Megan hadn't called her sooner, horror at what could have happened given how drunk she was, and relief that nothing worse had happened.

"If you pay me for working here, I could buy a new phone," Megan suggested, as they pulled past the gatehouse and onto the estate.

Lucy didn't bother answering. They both knew she'd get Megan a new phone—Lucy was too protective not to make sure Megan had a means of constant communication. Not that it had helped much last night. Maybe she'd get her one of those old-fashioned flip phones they advertised for seniors, the kind that barely even sent texts. Load it with tracking software Megan couldn't circumnavigate. The thought lightened her mood a bit.

She parked beside Wash's van. Megan lowered her head to look over the tops of her sunglasses. "This is where you work?"

The ancient Queen Anne-style mansion was the ancestral home of the Fraziers—among the first white settlers in western Pennsylvania, they'd established a trading post here, fought alongside the Iroquois against the British, and had saved countless from the treacherous falls beyond the bluff where the mansion stood with the warning beacon they'd kept lit. Now the Beacon Group worked here as a non-profit, assisting law enforcement to identify missing persons and solve cold cases local authorities didn't have the resources to handle. Few people understood that—particularly in small, rural jurisdictions suffering from budget cuts—it was much too easy to get away with murder, despite the police's best efforts.

When the police or families of victims hit a dead end in their quest for justice, they came to the Beacon Group. In the past few years the requests for assistance had exploded, leading the Beacon Group to hire Lucy to coordinate their field investigations.

Lucy got out of the car, tempted to slam the door, but instead cradled it shut with the palm of her hand, mindful of Megan's hangover. When she looked up, an elegant black woman with silver hair was approaching from the mansion's front door: Valencia Frazier, owner of the Beacon Group.

"She looks a little young for a recruit," Valencia said, appraising Megan. "Not to mention a little worse for wear."

Lucy had called Valencia this morning and explained the situation, planning to take the day off. It had been Valencia who'd suggested Megan might appreciate the consequences of her actions after a day or two spent working with the Beacon Group.

"Especially the case we have coming in," she'd added. "It deals with all the worst things that could happen after an evening of drinking and poor judgment."

"Nothing sexual?" Lucy asked. Megan had

already learned way too much about sexual violence, despite Lucy's over-protective nature; too many of her FBI cases had made it to the headlines, complete with salacious, graphic details.

Lucy sometimes worried she'd scarred her daughter by simply doing her job—even though she tried her best to leave work at the office and keep her home a safe haven. Still, work always seemed to spill over those barriers, including a hit man killing Lucy's mother and almost killing Nick and Megan. That had been in January, six months ago. Lucy had been injured and was still rehabbing her ankle—the official reason for her leaving the FBI—but it was working through the grief and guilt that swamped her when she least expected it that was truly difficult.

"Nothing sexual, at least not from the records I've received," Valencia had told her. "But one boy left dead and another who lost an eye. Just because of a few drinks too many and poor judgment. The perpetrator was a girl about Megan's age."

This morning Lucy had run the idea past

Nick, and he'd said a little tough love wouldn't hurt, but she still wasn't convinced. She hated the idea of involving Megan in her work, even if it was to teach her a life lesson. But she'd decided to give it a try—Megan would spend the day filing and scanning the paperwork that accompanied cold cases; at least she wouldn't be left home alone.

Lucy made the introductions. "Valencia Frazier, this is my daughter, Megan Callahan." They had given Megan Nick's surname; another way of distancing her family from Lucy's work. "You wouldn't know it to look at her now, but she's pretty good with the alphabet. I was thinking a few days in the file room?"

Megan rolled her eyes so high Lucy could see them above the rim of her sunglasses. "If I'm stuck here all day, couldn't I do something not so boring?"

Valencia took Megan's arm. "We'll see, young lady. Your mother has entrusted you to my care for the day. How about we start with a tour, and you can tell me all about yourself?"

As the two walked away, headed toward

the bluff with its spectacular views, Valencia glanced back at Lucy and gave her a smile. Megan was in good hands. Lucy watched until they turned the corner and left her sight, and then headed inside to greet her team.

Chapter 4

I KNEW IT WOULD TAKE the county sheriffs a while to get over the mountain in the storm, but our volunteer fire department is better than the ones in most big cities. Over the years, they've saved our little unincorporated hamlet from dozens of fires stupid hikers and weekend nature lovers accidentally set while visiting the national forest. Since the nearest hospital is over in Cleveland, they also run the ambulance crew. Good thing, because our population is skewed to both sides of the bell curve: very young and very old. Between the war and the unemployment and the lure of meth, an entire generation in between has vanished. My mom and dad included.

I don't know how long I sat there, holding Jack's hands, unable to do anything to help him except lie about Hank being okay. I couldn't risk putting pressure on his wound—the eyeball was clearly gone, but what if that was his actual brain beneath the burble of blood, and I hurt him more? I wiped the blood away before it could trail into his mouth or ear and tried to talk to him, keep him from going into shock; told him everything was going to be all right. The CD ended, abandoning us to a silence so deep I wasn't sure I'd ever climb out again.

Jack mostly babbled—talking about the football game tomorrow night, about how mad his dad would be when he found out he and Hank had stolen his gun and booze, asked me to hide his and Hank's drugs, kept telling me not to let his mom see him like this... Finally sirens sounded, the storm still strong enough that their wail was punctuated by the rattle of the tin roof above us. Jack squeezed my hands tight, pulling me down to his ruined face, his good eye rolling around until finally it focused on me. "We was only trying to have a bit of fun. Why'd you do it, Cherry?"

His words burned like acid. I pulled back so hard his bloody grip on my arm slipped and I went flying back, jostling him. A moan escaped him just as the firemen thundered inside. The firefighters—men I'd known my entire life—stared at me like I was a thousand miles away, too small and insignificant for them to take notice of. They swarmed over the room, checking on Hank; a quick shake of the head from one of the medics and they hustled their equipment over to Jack, separated me from him, their radios crackling as they called the hospital. One of them—a teacher from the elementary school who once upon a time had taught me my times tables—checked me over for injuries, then used his bulk to keep me in the far corner where I couldn't see past him as his partners worked.

It was all over so fast—and suddenly I was left with my old math teacher and two more firemen who covered Hank with a yellow plastic tarp. Jack was gone, on his way to the hospital in

Cleveland, most likely heading from there to the trauma center in Chattanooga. The men talked quietly, never making eye contact with me except when I moved toward the dingy bathroom, hoping to start scrubbing myself clean of the stench of blood and vomit and piss—Jack's, not mine—and gun powder.

"You need to wait," my old teacher told me, his hand on my arm but his gaze aimed high above my head, never meeting my eyes. "The sheriff will be here soon."

"Wait?" My mind hadn't made it past his first sentence—it was like swimming through mud, his words slipping away faster than tadpoles. I rubbed my palms up and down the burn scars on my arms, but that only made a sticky mess, releasing more of that iron smell that made me gag.

"It's a crime scene, Cherish," he told me, his words slow enough for me to finally grasp. "You understand that, right?"

The smells and the throbbing in my head—from the booze or the rain pounding on the metal roof, I wasn't sure—the feel of half-dried blood, the chill of my wet clothes, the sight of blood slipping across the concrete floor to the drain, the bright yellow tarp turning Hank's body into an anonymous alien blob, the men in their firefighting gear all staring at me... I opened my mouth, wanting to scream, wanting to run, to hide, to leave this horror behind.

I did none of that. Instead, I did what I always did: remained silent and pushed myself deep into the shadows, hoping no one would notice me. Fading into nothing was always my best defense, one I'd learned after my dad left to go to war, when it was just me and Mom and her new "friends." I clamped my lips tight, throttling my screams, and huddled in the corner, making myself small, my eyes cast down like a wild animal caught in a trap, hoping that if I couldn't see them, they wouldn't see me.

After my dad went to war, when we still lived in the cabin—before it burned down and the police told us all the land was now forever contaminated because of the chemicals and they'd sent me to live with Gran—I'd used the skills Dad taught me when we went hunting to learn how to become invisible. The art of camouflage and silence.

I'd pushed my bed into the corner beneath the window, leaving only enough space for a skinny girl to slip between the mattress and the wall and vanish the instant the door opened and the light switched on. The area beneath the bed was filled with a carefully constructed obstacle course of toys and books designed to distract someone flying high on crystal while I hid, curled up in Dad's old sleeping bag, becoming part of the discarded debris of childhood. If it was warm enough, I'd change into tomorrow's school clothes, slip outside, and sleep in the woods until it was time to run for the bus. The wild animals of the forest felt far less dangerous than the wild men my mother invited into our home.

Tonight there was no escaping into the forest. I was trapped in a cinderblock cage, held captive by men who'd known me my entire life. The same men who'd been there to rake through the ashes of our cabin, who'd transported my mom and her friends to the burn center in Chattanooga, who'd then looked on me with pity. But there was no pity tonight. Not for me. Tonight their expressions were the same they'd showered on my mom after the fire: disgust and anger, barely hidden behind masks of bland, self-righteous superiority.

Then the front door banged open, its metal colliding with the cinderblock wall so furiously I swear I saw sparks fly. Two men stepped inside, plastic coating their Smokey Bear hats, rain puddling in the creases. One was wearing a bright yellow slicker, its flap shoved back behind the holster of his gun. The other, the one leading the way, had no protection from the storm, yet his khaki uniform wasn't wet at all. His fierce expression implied it was because mere raindrops would never dare to defy him.

"We got it, boys," he told the firemen.

They filed out, and my old teacher paused at the threshold to talk with the second deputy for a moment. Then the office was empty except for the two deputies at the door and me in the farthest corner, Hank's body lying between us. The second deputy closed the door, and a hollow silence thudded between us, a silence that contained my entire life within its steel-knuckled grasp.

"Jasper, start documenting the scene," khaki deputy told his rain-slicker partner. "And for God's sake, don't contaminate it any more than it already has been."

Jasper nodded and pulled out a small disposable camera and began snapping pictures. On TV they would have had a special crime scene photographer with video and lasers and infrared and everything else fancy equipment. Not here. Craven County may be large, geographically, extending out to the Tennessee/North Carolina border and all the way south to Georgia, with the Nantahala National Forest spilling past our eastern boundaries, but tax base-wise, it's tiny, with barely enough money to keep the schools—two elementary, one middle, and one high school—and other essential services running.

Jasper reached me and stopped. "What about her?"

Khaki deputy drew close enough that I

could read his brightly polished name tag—Warren. The way he moved, his posture, his gaze that never stopped searching for hidden dangers, reminded me of my dad. Warren had also been a soldier, I'd bet anything. It was in his eyes. Now those eyes came to focus on me. And they did not like what they saw.

"She's evidence. Document what you can, then I'll take her to the station and do the rest."

Thunder rumbled, shaking the tin roof. Jasper jumped, his fingers clenching so that he took a picture of his own boot while almost dropping the camera. "You know what they used to use this place for?" he asked. "Maybe we should take her down to the station first, take the pictures there."

"Afraid of butchered cow ghosts?" Warren chuckled. "Or is it the rumors of all the revenue men and other carpetbaggers disposed of around here?" He took the camera, ratcheted the small plastic wheel, and clicked the button, the flash blaring in my face, over and over, walking a full circle around me until he was satisfied. "That'll do for now. We'll document any injuries and the rest at the station."

"She's a minor. Reeks of alcohol. We should take her to the hospital for a tox screen."

Warren pushed his face inches away from mine. I'm not sure how, but I managed to meet his gaze. It was like staring into a mineshaft—dark and empty.

"Seems sober enough to me. What do you say?" He still didn't call me by name, as if I didn't deserve one. "Want to go to the hospital? Get checked out? Pull the doctors trying to save your friend's life away from him? Meet his family, tell them what went on here, how their other son is lying dead in the dirt?"

I cringed and shook my head. The thought of seeing Jack and Hank's parents almost had me retching again.

"Thought so." He took my arm, spun me around, and before I could look back to see what he was doing, two metal bracelets snapped around my wrists. The handcuffs were tight; they pinched my skin and rubbed against knobby wrist bones and the scars snaking along my forearms, but the pain was nothing to the crushing realization that this wasn't a nightmare I'd wake up from or a midnight fear I could hide from.

As we trudged past Hank's body, Jasper opened the door for us. The wind fluttered the yellow tarp, raising one corner of the makeshift shroud. Hank stared up at me, and his eyes didn't seem empty at all. Instead they blazed white-hot hatred. At me.

Chapter 5

LUCY'S TEAM HAD THEIR WORKING SPACE on the mansion's second floor in a converted bedroom suite. TK O'Connor was already there, telling Wash, their tech analyst, a story from her days as a Marine MP. She told those stories a lot—usually tales of fresh recruits far from home, their good judgment obliterated by alcohol—but Lucy had noticed that although TK made the situations sound funny, the stories were more about universal human foibles than making fun of her fellow Marines.

She'd also noticed that TK never told stories about her other duties, when she served on a Female Engagement Team, going on front-line missions with special ops squads. TK had won medals and citations for those missions, had been caught in firefights and close quarters combat situations, had saved lives and taken lives and risked her own more than once; but whenever asked, she'd merely shake her blonde curls, making her look like a teenager instead of the mid-twenties woman she was, hiding her eyes along with their haunted expression, and change the subject.

Lucy knew from first-hand experience that talking helped—of course, it was easy for her since she had Nick to listen to her—and occasionally worried about TK. When she'd first met the former Marine, TK had been living in a barren room that resembled nothing more than a monastery cell. During these past few months TK had emerged from her self-imposed exile, moving into Valencia's gatehouse, enrolling in college courses, and starting counseling at the VA. She'd also met a guy, David Ruiz, and even though they were juggling a long-distance romance and David had issues of his own, Lucy could tell they were good together. Solid.

TK came to the punch line. "So of course we confiscated the pig and put it in the cell right beside him."

"And then what?" Wash asked. "Did the pig get convicted?"

"Sentenced to death—best barbeque we had all summer."

Wash laughed, his wheelchair bouncing. He was the youngest of the team, only in his early twenties, but in many ways they couldn't function without him. Not only were his cyber-skills and tenacity invaluable, but Wash could also look at a problem differently than the rest of them, seeing all sides, analyzing and probing until he found a way to crack it. After a drive-by shooting when he was twelve had left him paralyzed from the waist down, he'd had way too much experience cracking problems and removing obstacles.

Megan could learn a lot from both Wash and TK. "Where's Tommy?" Lucy asked. Tommy Worth was the final member of her team, a former pediatric ER physician and victim's advocate who'd joined the Beacon

Group to provide medical expertise and also so he could have the regular hours he needed to raise his daughter after his wife's murder. "Megan is joining us today and I'd love for you all to maybe let her know it's not cool to get drunk at parties in the middle of nowhere with older kids around."

They glanced up at her. "Of course it's cool," TK said. "It's just not smart."

"Tommy's on vacation," Wash put in, answering her original question. "Gone all week."

"Right. I forgot." Lucy took her seat at the antique dining room table that served as their work area. "Valencia is giving Megan a tour, but she thought this case might be a good one to serve as a life lesson."

"Lucy, seriously. If she was that drunk, then the hangover and embarrassment are lesson enough." TK moved to take her own seat across from Lucy. "Trust me. Been there, done that."

"You didn't see the guys there. Most of them Megan's known for years, but get a little beer in them and they turn into—" Lucy broke off, the image of the boy she'd found with Megan last night haunting her.

"They turn into guys," Wash supplied. "Young, stupid, and horny. I'm sure nothing would have happened. And not all guys are like that, like the men you used to chase after when you were in the FBI. There are good guys out there as well."

"They seemed in short supply last night. At least when I got there."

TK and Wash exchanged a glance. "You crashed the party?"

"What was I supposed to do? She was out past her curfew, not answering her phone—of course I crashed it. And I called the cops."

TK shook her head as if Lucy had done the unimaginable. "Lucy, Lucy, Lucy. So not cool. I'll talk with Megan and try to convince her to forgive you."

"Wait until you have kids," Lucy snapped, tired of being treated like the bad guy.

Wash snorted a laugh at that. Both women turned to stare at him. "What?" Lucy asked.

"Nothing." He swept his hand over his mouth, trying to sober up but then chuckled again. "Sorry. Just picturing TK with kids. Pregnant, waddling around, chasing after a bunch of rug rats, shouting orders at them like a drill sergeant."

"I'd make a damned fine mother," TK retorted.

"Yeah, I'll put you down for khaki and camo diapers on your baby registry." He snickered despite TK's glare.

A knock at the door interrupted them. "Excuse me, the receptionist said to come up," said a man in his late twenties to early thirties, in a refined southern drawl that was slightly less pronounced than TK's West Virginia accent. "I'm JH McCabe, from Justice for Youth."

Lucy sprang to her feet. "Mr. McCabe, of course. You're early. Please, have a seat."

McCabe joined them, swinging a black attaché case onto the antique table with such force that Lucy feared its Queen Anne legs would buckle. He was dressed in a conservative navy suit with strictly tailored lines, a crisp white shirt that even the July heat and humidity hadn't dared to wrinkle, and a bold red tie, the kind advertised as a "power" accessory. The attaché case was polished like new and its lock opened with a satisfying snap of brass on brass.

"Thank you," he said, finally sitting down, the open briefcase angled so he could reach its contents at a moment's notice. He withdrew a shiny silver card case from his breast pocket and dealt each of them one of his business cards, his movements rigid and precise. "As you know, this case has been an extremely frustrating one. Miscarriage after miscarriage of justice multiplied and compounded through the years." He sounded as if he were giving a jury summation. "With one child paying the price."

Wash and TK nodded—of course, they hadn't been gallivanting about the countryside searching for their wayward daughter last night. Instead, they'd been reading the case materials like Lucy should have been. She leaned forward, her hands clasped together on the table in an earnest fashion. "Please, Mr. McCabe. Tell us about the case. We'd love to hear it all, in your own words."

He blinked, startled. "Isn't that a waste of time? After so much of it has been lost already?"

"No, not at all," she countered, ignoring TK's smirk as the younger woman realized Lucy had been caught unprepared. "Hearing it from you rather than relying on the distilled notes from the case file will help paint the picture—create context."

He considered it, frowned, then said, "Context. Yes. Very well. If it will aid in your efforts to locate Cherish Walker."

Wash took his cue and clicked a key on his computer to project a school photo of a teenager with front teeth that overlapped the slightest bit, long brown hair, freckles, and eyes that didn't rise up to meet the camera. McCabe angled his chair away from the image on the screen at the opposite end of the room, choosing to focus on Lucy and her team.

"Cherish Anne Walker, age fourteen when taken into custody for the death of Henry Simon Kutler and the attempted murder of his twin brother John Michael Kutler, both aged eighteen."

Another photo appeared, this one of twin teens dressed in football uniforms, one kneeling in the classic Heisman pose, the other standing, arm cocked back as if throwing a football.

"The crime took place in October, 2006 at the Kutler family's farm. Drugs and alcohol, along with the murder weapon, a .45-caliber semiautomatic Taurus pistol, were found at the scene." McCabe's tone was distant, as if the facts he was reciting had nothing to do with the fates of three kids. "When police arrived, Henry Kutler was DOA, killed by a close proximity gunshot to the face and head, while John Kutler had suffered a gunshot to his right eye and was barely conscious. He later recovered, although he lost the eye."

"Those are the facts," Lucy interrupted his dry litany. "But what's the story behind them? Did the kids know each other? Why was Cherish there? Whose weapon was it?"

"What about the drugs and alcohol? Who did they belong to?" Wash asked. "Were the kids intoxicated?"

"Two older guys and a girl," TK said. "Any evidence of sexual assault?"

McCabe frowned at them. "It doesn't matter what happened that night—you can twist the evidence any way you want. John Kutler told the police that Cherish Walker shot him, and when his brother tried to wrestle the gun away from her, she shot and killed Henry. Cherish claimed she was the one trying to get the gun away from Henry after Henry shot his brother. The forensic evidence doesn't prove or disprove either version. Yet we still have one boy maimed for life and another boy dead."

"And the girl blamed for all this has been on the run for over a decade," Lucy said, skimming through the reports she should have read last night. "After being charged as an adult and escaping custody." She glanced up. "Surely this is a job for the US Marshals?"

"They've gotten nowhere, and now they're off the case."

"Off the case?" She scrolled down on her laptop's screen, only to encounter massive blocks of text filled with legal jargon at the very end of the case file.

"It's no longer their jurisdiction," McCabe explained. "Because in the eyes of the law, Cherish Walker is no longer a fugitive. Thanks to the Supreme Court's recent rulings and a review of her case, Justice for Youth was able to get the original charges against her dismissed."

TK looked puzzled. "Then why are we here?"

"We're here because Cherish Walker has no idea that she's now free." McCabe's tone grew strident, as if he were desperate to convince a jury. "She has no clue that she can return to her life any time she wants. Because no one can find her to tell her that her life is hers once more. She's gone dark, so deep underground that no one has any idea where to even begin looking. And she'll stay there, living as a hunted, wanted criminal, hiding in the underworld of society's shadow, unless you find her."

CHAPTER 6

MEGAN'S HEAD CLEARED AS SHE and Valencia strolled along the bluff. If she looked upriver, she could see all the way to Pittsburgh; glancing the other direction, she could follow the Monongahela as it streamed past farmlands until it vanished around the steep bend leading to the waterfalls. The vista was spectacular, like something out of a movie—an illusion heightened by the pair of hawks soaring overhead and the way the light shimmered in the July humidity. She really could imagine settlers here, working alongside the natives, searching for game in the thick forest surrounding the estate or braving the rapids of the river below.

"I've never seen your mother so frightened," Valencia said.

Megan shrugged a shoulder. "I have. And she's not frightened. More like angry and disappointed. Even though I didn't do anything."

"So you weren't drinking?"

"It was rum and Coke. Not like smoking pot—even though that's almost legal."

"Almost legal doesn't count. Your mom said some of the kids were doing other drugs."

"Not me. And she knows that. She just expects me to always be the perfect one, the one who never screws up, who follows the rules—it was even worse when she was still in the FBI. I couldn't even look at a boy without her running a background check."

Valencia steered them into the garden, where shade trees provided relief from the sun—and Megan's pounding headache. The air was scented with roses and lilies. "What would you do differently if you were a parent?"

The question surprised Megan. No one had

ever asked her anything like it before, not even her dad. "I would have trusted my kid to do the right thing."

"Which is exactly why your mom let you go to the party in the first place, right?"

"Yeah, but—I'm not a baby. I didn't need rescuing." Megan slumped down onto a nearby bench. "I was so embarrassed. Bad enough she came for me and Emma, but then she called the cops. I'll never be able to show my face again—and this year is the first year I'll be able to go out for varsity. As if anyone would want me on their team after last night."

"So your life is basically ruined by your mother's one bad decision?"

Megan sighed. "No. That's not fair. I should have called her—and I would have, if stupid Dylan hadn't thrown me and my phone in the pool."

What made it even worse was that stupid Dylan was the only reason she'd wanted to go to that stupid party in the first place. None of those kids were her friends other than Emma—but she'd had a crush on Dylan all year. Not that he'd ever even looked at her before last night. Her cheeks burned. Not that he'd ever even look at her again except to laugh at her.

"I had a feeling there was a boy involved," Valencia said. "Let me guess: Dylan is a bit older than you? Probably told you that you were old enough to have a little rum mixed into your cola?"

Megan nodded, her eyes closed behind the shelter of her sunglasses. "It was stupid. I was stupid to think—" She sniffed. "Anyway, it wasn't me he was interested in. He was just using me to get to Emma. God, she was so wasted, she was ready to—" She broke off. It wasn't her place to betray Emma's confidence, even if Emma had been so drunk she wouldn't remember how Dylan had grabbed her and pushed Megan—and her phone—into the pool when Megan tried to stop him. But Megan would never forget the way Dylan and all his friends had laughed at her. Including Emma.

They sat in silence for a few minutes, something she never could have done with her mom. Lucy was much too restless to sit still—

always had to be somewhere, doing something, solving someone's problems. Sometimes she wore Megan out. Sitting here with Valencia was kind of nice, even if it did make her miss her grams. She blinked hard; sometimes thinking of Grams and how she died still made her cry.

Finally Valencia asked, "Do you want to go inside and talk to your mother?"

"No." Megan leaned back, enjoying the sensation of the breeze shifting the flowers' fragrances around her. "You said this case she's working on is about a girl my age?"

"Younger, even."

"What happened? Was she—" Megan let Valencia fill in the blanks of all the terrible things that could have happened to girls featuring in any case Lucy worked on. Girls she'd been competing with all her life. Victims.

Megan was no victim. She was working on a black belt in Kempo and a purple belt in jujitsu, and she'd won marksmanship trophies for her shooting; a few months ago she'd delivered a baby while bad guys were chasing them down a mountain. Which should make her feel like the winner compared to the kids her mom was always being called away to help.

But somehow it never did. Lucy still left, and even though Megan knew her mom loved her more than anything, that she'd lay down her life to protect Megan and her dad, it didn't take the sting away. Especially when Megan's imagination filled in the blanks left by what little she heard about Lucy's cases, making those victims seem somehow prettier or nicer or smarter or more deserving of Lucy's attention than her own daughter.

Used to be she'd get angry or sulk when Lucy got caught up in a case. Or she'd work to be as independent as possible, telling herself it didn't matter if Lucy wasn't there, Megan didn't need her. But a chance to actually help? To be involved, not just watching from the sidelines, risking being run over when things went wrong like they had in January when her grams was killed?

"This girl wasn't killed or harmed," Valencia answered Megan's question. "Eleven years ago she was accused of shooting two people and escaped custody. We're trying to track her down."

The girl Lucy was searching for wasn't a victim but a villain? Even after screwing up last night, Megan could definitely win *that* competition. Plus, she could show Lucy she wasn't a baby, that she could be trusted. "Tell me about her case. What's her name?"

"Cherish. Cherish Walker."

CHAPTER 7

As Lucy listened to McCabe explain Justice for Youth's fight to have basic legal rights granted to juveniles, she couldn't help but dissect the way she'd reacted the night before with Megan. How on earth had her own mother put up with Lucy during those tumultuous adolescent years? Especially as they'd both been reeling with grief after the death of Lucy's father. Lucy had spent her adolescence stuck in the anger phase of mourning; blaming her mother, blaming her father, blaming herself. She'd acted out much worse than a few drinks at a party—it was a miracle she'd made it through those years alive, much less without getting arrested.

But her mother had never given up on her. Not even when Lucy hit her low point—a night partying with older boys that had somehow ended up with Lucy making out with two of them in the graveyard, where they would be assured of privacy. The only reason both boys hadn't mistaken her blurry, not-quite-black-out drunken come-ons as consent and had sex with her was that she'd thrown up on them, and they'd abandoned her to return to the party in search of other less noxious female companions. She'd woken the next morning half naked and sleeping in her own vomit on top of her father's grave. The fear and shame of that night had finally driven out her anger. Until last night, when all those feelings had come rushing back.

McCabe droned on and on about how children were routinely denied their rights without even being allowed to confer with their parents, let alone a lawyer. "Do you realize that the feds had to take over the juvenile system in Memphis because they refused children access to a defense attorney? Talk about a failure of due process!"

He waxed indignant about the ten-year-old in California who had waived his Miranda rights after shooting his abusive father but had no understanding what a 'right to be silent' was, much less the consequences of his actions. "He actually asked the arresting officer, 'How many lives do we each get?' Thought his dad would come back, like in the cartoons or video games."

According to McCabe, in Craven County, Tennessee, where Cherish Walker had been arrested, children still weren't always allowed access to a defense lawyer unless they—the children—agreed to pay for them. Unlike adults, who were given a public defender free of charge, juveniles were often denied that right by judges. All Lucy could think about was how unfairly she'd judged Megan last night. God, she wished it had been Nick there instead of her. He would have known exactly what to do and say.

"We understand how difficult it was for you to appeal Cherish Walker's case, Mr. McCabe," TK said, interrupting the attorney as well as Lucy's parental guilt fest. "But how does that help us to find her now? Today. Eleven years later."

McCabe blinked, closed the folder in front of him, and straightened it, but unable to align it with the curved edge of the table, he had to settle for using his briefcase as an anchor point instead.

"She was fourteen when she escaped custody," Lucy said. "Her only known family, her grandmother, had just died. So who did she know? Who might have helped her? Where would she have gone? If we can trace those early steps, it might help us to find where she went from there." The state police and local law enforcement would have covered the same ground, but you had to start somewhere.

McCabe cleared his throat, mentally shifting gears from his dissertation on legal theory to messier real life facts. "It's all in the reports. Other than the courthouse security officer, no one reported speaking to her that day—at the courthouse, in the transport van, or the juvenile detention center. The staff all said she was quiet, kept to herself, didn't draw attention. Which is exactly how she escaped. No way she could have planned it. It was her first appearance in adult court. She had to change into civilian clothing so the potential jurors wouldn't prejudge her. It's a rural county in the mountains east of Chattanooga—they weren't used to dealing with juvenile prisoners, especially not young girls. The guard let her use a private bathroom to change in while he stood outside. But there was a disturbance down the hall—a man attacking a girlfriend who was there to take out a restraining order. The guard only turned his back for a minute, he says, but she was gone. Walked right out the door. No one even noticed her. And she hasn't been seen since."

"No one that the investigators spoke to has seen her," Wash put in. McCabe's gaze jerked over to where Wash was sitting behind his computers. "I mean, she doesn't have a cloak of invisibility. People have seen her and spoken to her. We just need to find the right ones."

"Exactly why I'm here." McCabe was older than Wash by only five or six years, yet his tone dripped with disdain. "You're the experts.

Although if the federal marshals and state police couldn't find any witnesses, I'd love to hear how you intend to."

Which brought everyone's attention back to Lucy. Who was still leafing through the file, searching for a lead that hadn't already been trampled into dust. She looked up, met McCabe's gaze, and smiled. "We'll start by talking to the other people no one seemed to notice—the people you've been fighting to give a voice to. The other kids housed in the detention center."

"Why?" McCabe asked, a note of irritation in his voice. "I just explained that the escape was a spontaneous opportunity, not planned. Which means she wouldn't have confided anything of interest to her fellow inmates."

"They lived with her for months. And if they don't know anything, we'll talk to the people in school with her, at her church, her neighbors, anyone who knew her."

TK leaned forward. "You mean treat her like a victim. Build a psychological profile of how she came to be there that night so you can understand what she'd do after she escaped."

McCabe bristled at that. "She may have been released on a technicality, but she's no victim."

"You said her charges were dismissed," TK said.

"Without prejudice. Which means the prosecutor can retry her if he chooses. Although he won't be able to use anything from her confession since the judge threw that out. But there's plenty of other evidence against Cherish Walker."

"Like her prints on the gun and John Kutler, the eyewitness," Wash put in. McCabe glared at him and he regrouped. "Sorry, no pun intended. The testimony of the surviving witness, I should say." Then he paused. "He is still alive, right? Recovered from being shot in the face like that—could he even testify, or does he have brain damage?"

"Of course he's alive," McCabe snapped. "Last I saw John Kutler, he was a productive member of society, following in his father's footsteps, taking over the family business." A hint of a smile edged through his stern expression. "Unlike Cherish Walker. You need to keep that in mind. She's not the victim here. She's a fugitive from justice."

"That your organization worked to free?" TK retorted. She leaned back, her arms crossed over her chest, obviously not as enthusiastic about this case as she had been.

"Cherish Walker was denied her constitutional rights. Justice for Youth worked to rectify that miscarriage of justice, and in so doing helped to change the system for *all* juvenile offenders. Thanks to us, in rural counties like Craven County, public defenders are now mandated to meet with clients before a juvenile can decide to waive their Miranda rights—that way, at least they'll be waiving them with full knowledge. Police are being trained in non-coercive, age-appropriate interview techniques. Cherish Walker's case has helped change juvenile law throughout the state. Soon maybe even the country."

"But you want us to bring her back to face a trial for murder?" TK asked. Her tone was sharp enough that Lucy glanced at her. TK ignored her to exchange glares with McCabe.

"We're not law enforcement," Lucy intervened. "We can't force anyone to go anywhere. But we can hopefully locate Cherish and let her know that for now the charges have been dismissed and she's free to live her life."

A strange shudder rolled through McCabe, and he forced his attention away from TK and back to Lucy. The lawyer seemed passionate enough about the legal challenges he'd conquered but not as comfortable dealing with real life people and their inexplicable, inconvenient lives. "Exactly. Once you find her, you'll put me in contact with her, and I can explain her legal options and advise her on a course of action. And finally, after all these years, justice will be served."

Chapter 8

While Deputy Warren restrained me in the back seat of his police car, enough rain sliced inside the cruiser to leave puddles in the contours of the plastic seat. Despite the seat belt he fastened around my body, with my hands cuffed behind my back, I was helpless to keep from slipping with each swerve and curve and bump in the road. Adding to my misery was the stench swaddling me like a wet towel, threatening to choke my every breath. By the time we left the valley and turned onto the highway leading to the sheriff's station, I'd collapsed into a shivering, drenched, cramped, bruised shadow of a girl.

I didn't care about any of that. My suffering paled in comparison to what Jack and his family were going through. As the car sloshed its way through the storm, I took advantage of the quiet and the darkness that cloaked the rear compartment and finally allowed my tears to flow. My memory was still muddy, but flashes had returned, lightning strikes of brilliant clarity that revealed my guilt. *All my fault,* was all I could think as I sobbed silently, my face turned away from Warren and toward the window, facing the storm outside.

When we finally reached the station, a beige stucco building that also housed our post office and government offices, Warren removed me from the car without a word. He hadn't spoken to me at all the entire trip but had simply glowered at me occasionally in the rearview mirror. He escorted me inside to a small room with no furniture except a steel bench along one wall with a railing above it and a sliding window like in a dentist's reception area. Depositing me on the bench, he moved my handcuffs so that my left wrist was free and the right one was now attached to the railing, and then he flicked a few errant raindrops from his shoulders and strode to the window. "Got one for processing. Female. Did a pat down, but she'll need a full body, plus photos and evidence collection. The detectives leave for the scene? Or do they want to start with her?"

A man's voice, presumably a desk sergeant sitting beyond the window, answered. "They're going to meet the coroner at the scene. Said you should wait here with the subject until they've had a chance to get your report."

He leaned against the window, rolling his eyes at me. "Sarge, can't the female duty officer stay with her? I left Jasper back there controlling the scene; he's going to need some help."

"You mean you want to get back there and work the scene with the detectives. I know you want to move up, Warren. So do they. But a case like this, you gotta be a team player. Would you rather join the Sheriff at the hospital, waiting with the boys' parents?"

"No, sir."

"Didn't think so."

Warren scowled at me from across the room until the interior door buzzed open and a female deputy entered. He nodded to her and went inside, leaving me with her. The rest was a whirlwind—not helped by the fact that my brain was still numb from whatever Hank had given me to drink. I was beginning to wonder if maybe there'd been more than vodka in that orange juice. I felt so very far away from my body and the rest of the world, like if I stretched my free arm as far as it could go, I wasn't sure I'd ever reach the wall I was leaning against.

When I closed my eyes against the vertigo, my world filled with bloody visions—not just Jack and Hank, but Gran and my mom as well. Even after I opened my eyes and stared at the stark fluorescent light overhead, long enough for tears to blur everything blank, I still heard their screams. *All my fault...* Whatever happened from here on out, it was all my fault.

The lady deputy—I never did see her name clearly—led me to another featureless room where she made me stand on a paper sheet and undress. She took photos of every inch of my body, scraped beneath my fingernails, swabbed my hands, and after giving me a pair of white plastic overalls that swallowed me whole, took my mug shot pictures and fingerprints. She asked me about a possible sexual assault and I shook my head no—then I realized she was actually not talking to me but to Warren, who had joined us at the fingerprint station. "No signs of it on scene. If she's claiming it, we can send her for a rape kit after the detectives finish."

She shrugged and handed me back to Warren, wrinkling her nose at the stink still emanating from my tangled hair. He led me down the hall to an interview room with a table bolted to the floor and a plastic chair on either side. There was a railing across the table, and he attached my handcuffs to it. "The detectives will go over this again, but let's get Miranda out of the way."

It took me a minute to remember that Miranda wasn't a girl but the speech police gave you on all the TV shows and movies when they thought you were guilty and arrested you. In real life it was even more confusing. First he read from a card, and then he asked if I understood and said to sign and initial a piece of paper. I hesitated because I understood the words but not what they actually meant.

He leaned over me as I studied the form. "We can't move forward until we get this sorted. You do want to tell us your side of things, don't you, Cherish? Make everything right? For everyone?"

What I wanted was for Hank to be alive and Jack to be fine and my gran and mom to be home safe and sound and for my stomach to stop swishing and swirling and for this night to have never happened. My silence lengthened as I tapped the felt tip pen against one line of the form.

"You want an attorney?" Warren asked, a whiff of disappointment coloring his tone. "You sure? The county only has two juvenile defenders, so it will take time to get one here— probably not until tomorrow at the earliest. Do you think it's fair for Mr. and Mrs. Kutler to wait that long to know what happened to their boys? Oh, and the juvenile court judge charges kids for county defenders. Thinks it's part of their learning to be responsible."

I jerked my head up at that. With Gran in the hospital and not working, I'd scrounged all our cash to pay this month's rent on the trailer. "It says an attorney will be provided free of charge." They were my first words since we'd arrived, and my voice sounded strange—watery and weak, like the storm had washed most of it away.

"That's for adults." He shrugged. "Juvenile court is a whole different ballgame—the judge has the power to decide whatever he wants."

Acid etched my throat as I swallowed, trying to clear my brain enough to do the math. "How much?"

"For a lawyer? I dunno, probably three-fifty, four hundred." He sensed my distress and twisted the knife. "Per hour. That's if you don't go to trial, of course. And if you're not charged as an adult. But once you agree to talk to us, we might be able to get this all sorted out without getting the judge or lawyers involved. You know, if it was an accident or something."

I wasn't stupid. I knew he was trying to wear me down, acting like he was on my side, like he thought I was innocent. Even if I was, it was still all my fault—where did that fit into the black and white of the law?

"So...do you want an attorney? Or do you want to talk? Tell me what happened?"

It seemed like what I wanted had no place here. It felt so wrong, so very wrong. He stared at me, waiting, his expression urging me to follow his lead like a good little girl. To not give him any trouble, make waves, create complications. My stomach churned, and the iron blood scent made my head reel. My secret weapon had always been my ability to hide in silence. But that obviously wouldn't work, not here in the glare of the harsh lights reflecting from my white jumpsuit and the metal table. I felt naked and exposed. And out of options.

I hauled in a breath; it burned and scraped its way down my throat. I knew what I had to do...but could I do it? I signed the form and gave him back the pen. "I want to talk."

CHAPTER 9

IF TK HAD TO LISTEN TO MCCABE pontificate on the juvenile justice system for another minute she thought she might just scream. It wasn't that she didn't agree with the man—she did—but somehow he made every battle fought for the rights of kids sound as dry and dull as dog kibble.

"Hate to rain on your parade," TK put in, when he finally paused for breath. "But after all these years, are we even sure she's still alive?"

McCabe's jaw dropped and then clamped shut with an audible clack as he turned to glare at her. "I'm sure. She's out there. Somewhere."

TK exchanged a glance with Lucy.

McCabe's certainty wasn't exactly inspiring— was he wasting their time?

Wash, as always, was two steps ahead of everyone else. "I've been running Cherish's vital statistics through NamUs and the Doe Network; also NCMEC and the other missing persons databases. Nothing. If she's dead, no one has found her remains and entered her into the system."

At least enduring McCabe wasn't for nothing, then. "So," TK said, before McCabe could continue his legal diatribe, "since juvenile records are sealed, how do we find anyone who might have been at the detention center with Cherish Walker eleven years ago?"

"You said Craven County was rural; sparsely populated. Did they have more than one juvenile detention center?" Lucy asked McCabe.

He shook his head. "Just the one. Why?"

"How about schools? Can you give us the names of the high schools in the county?"

"There's only one of those as well. Craven High."

Lucy smiled and nodded to Wash. "Yearbooks," he said, fingers already typing. "Let's see—yes, they're online. Searching for anyone with a prolonged absence or who repeated a grade..." He glanced up. "Boys or girls?"

"Both," McCabe answered. "They would have been housed at the same facility."

TK knew what was coming next—she'd rather deal with the yearbooks than the tedium of personnel records. "Send the links to me and I'll do it," she volunteered.

"Okay. While TK finds us possible fellow detainees, along with classmates and teachers, Wash can start a search for any adults who might have had contact with Cherish while she was in custody—their names should be in her case files." Lucy glanced at McCabe. "I'm afraid this is where things get pretty boring, Mr. McCabe. Once we gather a list of potential witnesses to talk to, we'll schedule a trip to Tennessee—"

"Can't you just call them? Hurry things along a bit?"

"We do our initial interviews over the phone, but I've found in-person follow-ups are almost always more productive. Besides, it would be good to see where Cherish grew up—it would have informed her choices after she escaped."

"We should talk to the survivor, Jack Kutler," TK put in, as she scanned through smiling faces from the yearbooks. Had she ever been that young? She'd joined the Marines right after high school—had to, as they'd needed the money to pay her mom's hospital bills, and by then Mom had already been sick for years, leaving a mountain of debt that was crushing her father. No, she was pretty sure her yearbook photos didn't look as carefree as any of these kids.

"Why do you need to speak to Jack?" McCabe asked. "Surely that would be inappropriate. Not to mention insensitive and highly intrusive."

"We should at least see the crime scene," TK persisted, mostly just to see what new alliteration he came up with if she continued to irritate him. "Even if our job isn't to find evidence of Cherish's innocence, figuring out exactly what happened that night might help us find her."

"I don't see how," he said firmly. "Besides, all that ground has already been covered. You'd be wasting your time." By which he meant *his* time.

"Is Jack Kutler still living in Craven County?" Lucy asked.

"No. His parents divorced a year after his brother was killed, and Jack and his mother moved to Nashville."

"Maybe it will be enough to speak with his father, and see the crime scene."

"I'm really not sure all this is necessary," McCabe bristled. "It's not as if Cherish Walker would have ever gone anywhere near Craven County after her escape."

"Maybe not, but it's a starting point." Lucy scraped her chair back. "I'll see you out."

McCabe looked like he wasn't going to take the hint. But after a moment's hesitation he snapped his briefcase shut, spun it to face him, grabbed the handle, and stood. "Very well. I'll leave things in your hands. But I expect frequent progress reports. If you locate Cherish Walker, you need to contact me immediately. I must be there to explain the legal intricacies of her situation. Do not approach her without me."

TK glanced up at the sudden edge in his tone. Lucy did not like outsiders interfering in her cases or trying to give her orders—even if they were the client. But Lucy hid her rancor and simply nodded, saying, "I understand."

TK liked the way Lucy had agreed without actually agreeing or promising anything—and without making the situation worse by arguing, which would have been TK's initial impulse.

After Lucy and McCabe left, TK kept scanning the photos. Wash continued his typing and said, "You know I could import those into a database and make it go a lot faster."

"No, thanks. I like doing it the old-fashioned way." It actually wasn't that difficult since the website had a search function that allowed her to easily collate the student names by class. "Better than ferreting out work histories."

"Bet I'll finish before you."

TK had been on the losing end of Wash's sucker bets before. "No bet. Besides, what's the rush?"

"You didn't read McCabe's cover letter?"

"Tried to, but fell asleep it was so boring. Supreme Court this, Justice Department that, yada yada. I jumped right to the case files." Justice for Youth had documented not only Cherish's court battles but also their previous efforts to search for her after law enforcement had failed.

"He gave us a week—"

"Only a week? Why the deadline? They've been working on her case for years."

"Exactly. They're a nonprofit; they don't have the funding to keep searching for one client when they could be using that money to fight court cases that could impact hundreds or thousands of kids. They're trying to change the entire juvenile justice system."

He tapped his keyboard, and the projection screen at the end of the room lit up with the

Justice for Youth's website. "Look at the cases they're working on: abolishing solitary confinement for juveniles, ensuring adequate mental health and addiction treatment, mandating educational standards. And they've already helped to abolish life without parole—thanks to that Supreme Court ruling in 2012. Did you know that Pennsylvania had more kids locked up with life sentences than any other state in the country? And before that Supreme Court ruling, that the US was the *only* country in the entire world that sentenced kids to life without parole? The whole world!"

"Look who drank the Kool Aid."

He bounced the front wheels of his wheelchair against the hardwood floor. "Black kid growing up in Homewood, how many of my friends you think I've seen go to jail, do hard time, without anyone giving a shit about their rights, much less if they were actually guilty or not? Maybe they're not all saints, but I don't think making one mistake when your brain isn't even finished maturing should ruin your entire life."

"Cherish killed Hank Kutler," she argued. "And almost killed his brother. That definitely ruined Jack Kutler's life. Not to mention the rest of his family. Why shouldn't she have to pay for that?"

"I'm not saying she shouldn't. I'm just saying kids deserve a chance at a level playing field. McCabe is right about how the court system grinds kids down. It's an assembly line, destroying kids' lives. They can waive their rights without understanding them, they can get a lawyer who might not bother to meet them or even learn their name before their court date, they can get labeled and shuttled into a system that's all about saving money when it should be about saving lives. Like that judge who actually partnered with a few lawyers to buy a juvenile detention center and then they filled it with kids—many of them innocent—who came through his courtroom. Lining their pockets with kids' futures. Or what about when the juvenile courts are so overwhelmed they become a revolving door, with kids receiving no services until they really screw up and commit a felony—

or are accused of one—and get sent to adult court and real prison? So what good does that do anyone? Entire generations lost to a system that's meant to serve and protect them."

She raised an eyebrow. She'd never seen Wash so passionate about a subject—or so longwinded. "You don't think we should find her."

"No. I mean, yes, but—"

"You don't want her to get arrested and retried? Have her day in court?"

"Look where it got her the first time. Why should things be better now?"

Her screen filled with an image of Cherish's final school photo from the start of her freshman year. TK couldn't help but stare at the hope that brightened the girl's eyes despite her shy smile. So very different from the haunted desperation of her police booking photo taken only a few weeks later. "I know we're not getting paid to look into Cherish's case, but maybe we should? Just to verify things. I mean, who knows, maybe it will give us a lead to where she is now."

"McCabe won't like it."

"McCabe can suck an egg."

They both laughed, ducked their heads as Lucy returned with her daughter and Valencia, and got to work.

Chapter 10

Vomit dried my hair sticky, and I still stank of blood and death when we arrived at the Craven county juvenile detention center. Being pulled from the biggest crime scene the county had ever seen to ferry me through a raging storm had put Deputy Warren in a foul mood. After the detectives arrived and I repeated my story to them, he hadn't said a word—not even to ask me if I wanted to clean up or had to use the toilet or maybe needed water to rinse the foul taste from my mouth.

Now we were sitting in the parking lot of the detention center, a single-story cement and brick building that reminded me of my old middle school. The storm had gotten worse; enough so Warren deigned to put on his rain slicker before we left the sheriff's station. The rain and wind pummeled the police cruiser, and the flashing lights reflected back to us through the windshield in a washed-out kaleidoscope blur of color. Finally the door to the detention center opened, and an outside light flicked on.

Warren hopped out, his yellow rain slicker billowing in the gusting wind, and opened my door. He yanked me out, one hand protecting the top of my head since my hands were cuffed behind me, and pulled me down the cracked pavement leading to the door. They'd kept all my clothes at the police station, so I was still wearing the white overalls that were so big I had to hitch them up with my cuffed hands to keep from tripping. Blue elastic booties covered my feet, but they were worse than being barefoot, giving me no traction against the rain-slicked pavement.

By the time we reached the entrance where a bearded guy in his twenties was waiting, holding the door shut until the very last moment so he wouldn't risk getting wet, I didn't need that shower any more. The rain and wind had pretty much scoured me clean.

We entered a small office with fluorescent lights reflecting off white walls and a dented metal desk. Warren removed my handcuffs and told me to sit on the plastic chair against the wall and wait. The men sat at the desk and talked, at first business stuff, filling out forms and occasionally asking me questions like my gran's middle name and how much money she made a year and if my mom had ever bothered to sign over legal guardianship to Gran, along with anything else the police didn't already know.

Which wasn't much. Hartfield is a small town, surrounded by farmland on one side and the wilderness that is the Nantahala National Forest on the other. Even though I'd never been in trouble before, Warren was able to tell the detention worker who I was, where I lived, and my family history going back several generations, including the fact that my dad had died in Iraq and my mom had taken off soon after, running away with a meth-dealing biker. He acted like she was already dead.

Rainwater puddled at my feet. I was cold and scared and still half-drunk. I splashed the puddle with my toe, tracing silly cupid hearts. Hank and Cherish forever...he'd said he liked me, said he wanted to be my boyfriend...guess that wasn't ever going to happen now. I'd liked him—what girl wouldn't? But not Jack—he'd scared me, the way he watched without saying a word, his eyes roaming over my body like I belonged to him. As flattered as I was by Hank's attentions and words, it was Jack's silence that had made my stomach flutter—and not in a good way.

Back at the slaughterhouse, when Hank stopped talking long enough to refill my cup—he promised he wasn't spiking it, but if he hadn't, then Jack had—Jack sidled up and wrapped his arms around me, sliding one hand inside the back of my jeans, his palm sticky against my skin. He'd whispered things to me that were so horrid I didn't even hear the words, all I saw were terrible images filling every crevice of my brain. I'd gotten scared and shoved him, and he tripped over the coffee table, landing on his butt.

Hank had laughed so hard he sounded like a bull bellowing. I was trembling, trying to figure out how to get home with the storm and no bike, but Hank hugged me, his entire chest pressed so warm against mine, his hands gently teasing my goose-bumped skin, easing up both sides of my throat, tilting my chin until our lips touched... It was my first kiss ever, and I never wanted it to stop. I felt like a fairy-tale princess, and for one brief moment wasn't sure if my feet were even touching the ground.

Then Hank let me go. While I was trying to remember how to breathe, my fingers touching my lips, searching for the warmth he'd left behind, he raised a glass to toast Jack's clumsiness, insisting I drink the whole thing, holding the cup to my lips, his other arm wrapped around me as if we were forever connected, two halves of one body. He made me feel like there was no saying no to him because he had all the right answers, knew everything important in this world, including what was best for me.

"C'mon, Cherrygirl. You know you'll love it," he'd whispered, as he tugged my hair to tilt my head back until the entire red cup was drained. That's when everything got fuzzy.

Now in the too-bright intake office, I stopped my toe tapping and tried to concentrate. I didn't want to remember what came next. But I needed to remember, to understand exactly what had happened. I'd done the best I could with Warren and the detectives, but my story was so scattershot with holes that I could tell they didn't believe half of what I said. And I needed them to believe.

"Is Jack okay?" I asked Warren as he stood and shook his rain slicker, ready to leave me here. "Is there a way I can call him?"

"No." That was all he said. Then he was gone, vanished back into the night, swallowed by the storm.

The counselor—*Call me Brian*, he said— acted all sugary-nice, like he really wanted to help, but I'd noticed that he knew as much gossip about me and my family as Warren did. No one mentioned my dad's war medals or the way my gran worked two jobs or the fact that I'd made honor roll every semester except for fourth grade when the two soldiers came knocking with the news that Dad had been killed. No, we were all just Sunset Court trailer trash to them.

"I need to know," Brian asked, his pen hovering over a form, "are you or could you be pregnant?"

"No." I didn't bother to remind him I was only fourteen—I'd seen girls younger than me make that mistake. Funny how the guys who loved them so much never stuck around—and always blamed the girls, calling them sluts, saying they couldn't even be sure it was their kid or not.

That's when it hit me. Hank didn't like-like me. How could he? Just because I'd been watching his football exploits from the sidelines since I was little, there was no reason for him to have any idea who I was. He and Jack were eighteen, both seniors; I was only a freshman.

He didn't want to be with me, to take care of me. He'd wanted to have fun with me—would have probably let his creepy brother watch and then have his turn as well. God, how could I have been so stupid?

Anger finally burned away my shivering. I sat up straight, gathering the swaths of white plastic fabric overall into my fists.

"They didn't rape me," I told my new friend Brian. "I guess maybe they were going to, but it didn't go that far."

He gave a little shake of his head as if whisking my words away, his gaze never rising from the paper. "Didn't ask, and it's not for me to know or decide. That's on the courts. This is a medical history form, that's all."

He seemed more bored than interested as he droned on: "When was your last period? Any sexually transmitted diseases? Current medications? Allergies? Suicidal thoughts? History of self-harm?"

On and on it went until he had more of my life down on paper than anyone in the whole wide world. Finally he put his pen down, although I could see that there was still one last question on the form. Later I realized it was perhaps the most important question of all, but reading upside down across the desk I saw he'd already filled in the blank, answering it for me with a no: "Is there any reason why you feel as if your life might be in danger here?"

I frowned, trying to puzzle the reason behind the question, but he still wasn't watching me as he pushed the paper across the table. "Sign here and we'll get you a shower, some dry clothes, and a bed for tonight." He glanced at the clock: 4:40 in the morning. "Or what's left of it."

Scribbling my name, I looked at the phone beside the computer that he hadn't even bothered to turn on. It took all my courage to meet his gaze and ask, "When can I call my gran? When do I get to go home?"

He stood and gestured for me to stand and walk before him. "Remember these rules. You never walk behind a staff member, always in front where they can see you. You stop before any door and ask permission to enter. You never open a door on your own unless staff instructs you to. No touching or initiating any contact with staff. If you have a question, ask permission first, then you may speak."

We reached the door. I started to reach for the doorknob but remembered what he'd just told me and instead stood and waited.

"Say, *permission to cross*," he told me. It sounded strange, but I guess it made sense since it worked whether you were leaving or entering a room.

"Permission to cross," I intoned.

"Granted. Open the door."

I did as he instructed, and we continued down a featureless corridor with walls made of cement-block and painted that same shiny white that made the overhead lights bounce back and stab you right between the eyes.

"Excuse me, Brian," I said, not sure how to ask permission to ask something. "But when can I go home?"

At the end of the hall, another staff member opened a locked door and waited for us. Brian never answered my question as the two of them escorted me to a small room barely wide enough to hold a sink, toilet, and a cot.

I never saw home or my grandmother again.

Chapter 11

Her work at Beacon Falls wasn't as boring as Megan had feared, but no way would she ever admit that to her mother. While Lucy, TK, and Wash tracked down people who had known Cherish eleven years ago and did their initial phone interviews, Valencia gave Megan her own private office—it was the size of a broom closet, but she had her own computer and everything—and asked her to create a chronology of the initial evidence and compare it and the forensics to the original witness statements and police reports.

"Pretend you're the judge looking at all the evidence," Valencia had said. "It's your job to decide a person's fate."

"I thought that's what juries did?" Seemed like twelve people working together would have better luck than one person, even if that person did know the legal technicalities. Of course, lately all the news was filled with juries that couldn't get things right either.

"Not for juvenile cases," Valencia told her. "Just a judge. Unless he decides to move the defendant to adult court; then it can be either a judge or a full jury."

Huh. She hadn't known that. Was that better for kids or worse?

"When you're done, you can present your case to me. I'll see if it holds merit."

Megan had forgotten that Valencia had been a lawyer once upon a time. She was so stylish, dressed with such timeless elegance, that Megan sometimes forgot how old Valencia was—older than her grams, even. "So, if I convince you that Cherish is guilty, then what happens? How does that help you find her?"

"It doesn't, not directly. But in my experience, someone running because they're guilty—they never stop running."

"So if she was innocent, why didn't she turn herself in? Why did she run away at all?"

Valencia's smile reminded Megan of her dad's. "Good question. Let me know when you find an answer."

Megan spent the rest of the day organizing. There were papers—so many papers, despite the fact that the case was only eleven years old, so it wasn't like they didn't have computers back then—as well as computer files, some that duplicated the paperwork, others that were only on computer. In the end, she'd created two timelines with sticky notes telling her where to find the documentation: one following the events of the crime, the other how the investigation unfolded.

By the end of the day when her mom came to get her for their drive home, she wasn't satisfied with either timeline. Both had gaps, leaps of logic that made no sense, stories that contradicted each other, and very little hard evidence. In fact, the forensic evidence didn't point to any one person's guilt—not like on TV, although she knew from countless tirades from her mom when she used to have to testify and convince juries that real life wasn't like *CSI*. But still, she'd thought this case wouldn't be like that. After all, it was open and shut, right?

Cherish was guilty. Otherwise the juvenile judge wouldn't have sent her to adult court where she could be sentenced to spend the rest of her life in adult prison. In fact, that was the reason why Justice for Youth had gotten involved, not because they thought Cherish was innocent.

Plus, she ran. You didn't run if you were innocent. Cherish had to be guilty.

Megan mentally sifted through the facts as Lucy drove them home, trying to arrange them into a picture that made sense. She only wanted peace and quiet to think about everything, but Lucy had other ideas.

"Ready to talk about last night?" Lucy asked.

"Are you ready to listen?"

"Yes."

"I was trying to stop something bad from

happening."

"To you?"

"To Emma. She was drunk and high, and I thought, I was afraid, this boy was going to take advantage of her."

"Doesn't explain why you didn't just call me—or why Emma's parents didn't drive you home before your curfew like we'd arranged."

Megan shifted in her seat. "Emma told her parents you were driving." Lucy opened her mouth, her eyes tightening with judgment, but Megan kept going. "I didn't know until we were already at the party. Traci's mom was there, just like she told you she'd be, so I figured it would be no big deal, I'd just call you when we were ready to leave."

Lucy closed her mouth and nodded to Megan to continue. "But then after Traci's mom took everyone's car keys, she went to her room, and we didn't see her the rest of the night."

"Did she know about the keg? And the drugs?"

"She bought the keg. Traci said her mom says it's safer for kids to party at home instead of sneaking off to the woods or somewhere they could get hurt or drive drunk. Says we're all going to drink anyway, but at least this way she knows we're safe."

"Drunk, around a pool, hard liquor, drugs—" Lucy blew out her breath in exasperation.

"She didn't know about all that. Just the beer." At least as far as Megan could tell. "She didn't know about the older kids who showed up later either. I'm not even sure if all of them even go to our school."

"You should have called me sooner."

Megan took a deep breath. Why was talking to her mom always about what should have happened instead of what actually did happen? "Maybe. Yes. Okay. But I lost track of time—"

"You were drunk."

"I was having fun. At least at first. Then this guy started flirting with Emma and things went too far and I tried to pull her away and he, he—" Her cheeks burned as she remembered her humiliation.

"He did what? Megan, what did he do?" Lucy's speech grew rushed and Megan felt the tiniest surge of pleasure for making her fear the worst, even if it was only for a moment.

"He pushed me into the pool. That's why I couldn't call you." At least Lucy didn't laugh. Unlike Megan's so-called friends. "And then you came and got us and called the cops, and now I'll never be invited to another party for as long as I live."

"Not a problem since you're still grounded."

Seriously? Megan rolled her eyes and hunched in her seat. Had Lucy heard nothing? She'd done the right thing, tried to help a friend, only to pay the price.

Then Lucy reached across to squeeze her shoulder. "Grounded for the drinking," she amended. "Until your father gets home and we get a chance to discuss things. But despite that, I'm very proud of you. Standing up for your friend like that. Emma's lucky to have a friend like you."

Megan sighed. Not that Emma would ever

speak to her again after Lucy had brought her home drunk and made sure Emma's parents knew. "So now you know what really happened—and that it wasn't my fault."

"I never said it was your fault. I only said you needed to take responsibility for your actions."

"But you judged me before ever knowing what those actions were." Why couldn't Lucy understand? Her dad would have, if he were here. He would have listened, said something to cheer her up and make her laugh, and then they would have gone for ice cream or something fun. Not her mom. Lucy was all about consequences and learning lessons. "Is it because of this case? I'm not like Cherish Walker—not stupid enough to end up alone with two older guys or to grab a gun and start shooting at them."

"Megan Noel Callahan. You have no idea what really happened to that girl that night. No one does."

"Her fingerprints were on the gun and the kid who lost his eye saw her shoot his brother before he blacked out. After she shot him. He's lucky to be alive, his brother's dead, and her case gets thrown out on a technicality. What's fair about that? Where's the justice for the Kutler twins?"

"It's not my job to judge Cherish Walker, it's my job to find her."

Where was her mother, the crusader for victims young and old? What had this new job done to the passionate FBI agent Megan had once been so proud of? Lucy had only left the FBI to spend more time with her family—and to hopefully never again put them in the crosshairs of a killer like the man who'd murdered Grams. As much as Megan resented the time Lucy spent helping other kids instead of being with her, she'd never wanted her mother reduced to someone who just went to work because it was a job.

Then she realized—this wasn't about the case, it was about Megan and what happened last night. "I'll bet if Cherish was a guy and the two kids shot were girls, you wouldn't feel that way. You'd be all over the fact that a predator escaped custody. You'd do anything to find justice for those victims. To prevent the same thing from happening to anyone else."

Lucy was silent, a certain warning sign. Megan ignored it.

"How are you going feel," she asked, trying and failing to keep her tone neutral, "when you find Cherish Walker? Knowing that you're helping a killer go free?"

Chapter 12

"WORST THING ABOUT IT," Lucy told Nick later that evening as she sat alone, her laptop and case notes failing to fill the empty space on his side of the bed, "is she might be right." *She* being Megan, of course. "Cherish might be guilty. Probably. You should hear what the people in her hometown say about her." She'd spent all afternoon on the phone interviewing anyone they could locate who had known Cherish.

"Let me guess—she tortured animals, wet the bed, started fires, and threatened to kill anyone who got in her way?"

"No. Just the opposite. Her old teachers all

used almost the same words. Quiet. Never made a fuss. No one ever noticed her until the shootings."

"Ouch. What about the kids locked up with her?"

She sighed. This whole case was so damn depressing. "So far we haven't been able to find any of them to speak to. They're all gone."

"You mean moved out of the area?"

"I mean dead. Mostly from overdoses, a few car crashes. The ones we've found still living are in prison."

"Sounds like the odds are stacked against Cherish Walker. And against you finding her."

"At this point I feel more like a bounty hunter than an investigator. I don't understand why Justice for Youth is spending their money on this. I mean, granted, they can only afford a week—"

"Are you sure it's actually coming from them? Maybe this McCabe is paying out of his own pocket, and that's why the deadline. You said he was over-involved in this case."

She sat up, her laptop sliding off Nick's

pillow as she pulled the phone closer. "I hadn't thought of that. Maybe the deadline is because he's using his vacation as well? But why? I mean, if we find her, odds are she'll either go deeper underground, or sooner or later she'll be dragged back to Craven to face a murder trial. If he really cares about her, why do all this?"

"Was he involved in her case from the start? Maybe he feels like he let her down."

"No, he's only a few years older than she is. He would have been a kid himself back then." She paused, remembered the intensity that radiated off McCabe. "He wants to meet her." Not *want*—need? It felt right. Definitely put McCabe's behavior into better perspective. "Maybe he somehow thinks he's in love with her?"

"Like that Gene Tierney movie I always fall asleep during when you make me watch it? The one with the cop who falls in love with the murder victim's portrait."

"*Laura.*"

"You think he's obsessed with her?"

"Maybe. I'm not sure."

"Where's he from? Maybe he heard about the case when he was a kid."

"His accent is kinda Southern, but subtle, almost a non-accent. Like he's too smart and educated to have one. Not at all like the people from Craven County—at least not the ones we spoke to today."

"So not as distinctive as my gentlemanly Southern drawl," he said, in a parody of his own Virginian accent. "Or youns' Pittsburghese where you outen lights and read up your room and warsh your car."

She laughed and clamped her hand over her mouth. "I don't sound that bad."

"Bless my heart. Y'all just have no idea." Now he sounded exactly like his mother had the first time she'd met Lucy.

"Stop, stop." She wiped an errant tear away. "I have to get back to work. You'll be home tomorrow night? I might need to go to Craven myself, but Megan can wait at Beacon Falls. You can pick her up there."

"Yeah. They were worried that tropical storm in the Gulf would come this way, maybe delay flights out, but it looks like it's heading toward New Orleans."

She hadn't even checked the weather. Or the news. "Tropical storm?"

"Delilah. They said it might upgrade to a hurricane."

"But you're okay there in Florida?"

"We're fine. Other than the fact that it's a hundred degrees in the shade—I haven't even left the hotel."

"Not out carousing with the other trauma counselors? Swapping tales of PTSD over shots?"

"Speaking of carousing—"

"What are we going to do about Megan? I'm still not sure she's telling me the whole truth about everything that happened at that party."

"She's a kid. Did you tell your mother everything at that age?"

"Low blow." He knew she and her mother barely spoke when she was Megan's age. "But point taken."

"I'm just saying, don't interrogate her. She

knows she made a mistake—"

"More than one."

"Mistakes. But she also did the right thing to help Emma."

Except that was exactly where Lucy was pretty sure Megan was hiding the truth. Or part of the truth, at least. "Maybe you can get more out of her when you get home and I'm in Tennessee. She'll always talk to you more than me."

"It's my Southern charm." She could practically hear his smile. "Wait. That's why this case has you so upset. You *want* Cherish Walker to be innocent. Because if she didn't actually pull the trigger, if she's a victim instead of a killer, then somehow that means Megan—"

"I don't need you playing Dr. Freud and analyzing my neuroses to tell me that." Lucy couldn't help it. She always saw Megan in all of her victims—it's what gave her the strength and passion to fight for them. As if by saving them, she could build up enough good karma to protect her own family. Magical thinking, Nick called it. "It's not that I'd like Cherish to be innocent—in fact, it might be worse if she is. Because then if I do my job and find her, it's to tell her that even though she can go back to her old life, she'll probably still be arrested and face a new trial for Hank Kutler's murder."

"They can do that?"

"Sure, if the DA is feeling aggressive and wants an easy win or to score some PR points with the voters. With the little evidence there is, we have absolutely no idea what really happened that night, so the DA could spin it anyway he wanted. Good chance even if she is innocent, she'd be convicted and spend the rest of her life in prison."

"And if she's guilty?"

"If she's guilty, and I find her, she'll probably use the news to run farther, go so far underground no one will be able to bring her to justice."

"You're the one who always tells me that there isn't always a happy ending."

"No, but at least by doing my job, I wasn't making things worse. This time I feel like either way, I'll be the instrument of destruction, ruining a girl's life." She realized she definitely did not sound like the unbiased investigator McCabe was paying her to be. "Maybe I'll beg off. Tell Valencia that Megan needs me here."

"As if ignoring the problem is going to solve it?"

"It'd be someone else's problem." God, she sounded as whiny and petulant as Megan. "Forget I said anything. I'm just tired and frustrated."

"Frustrated?" he said, in a fake Freudian Viennese accent that somehow managed to sound sexy. "I see. Well, perhaps I can help with that, Madam. Tell me about your fantasies..."

CHAPTER 13

THE NEXT MORNING LUCY DROPPED Megan off early at Beacon Falls, picked up TK, and drove to the airport where Wash had booked them on the first shuttle to Atlanta. TK traveled light—her old Marine's rucksack her only luggage—and the car rental was prebooked and ready to go thanks to Wash, but once they arrived in Atlanta they still had to wait for Lucy's checked bag.

"Better than traveling naked," TK said, once they finally reached their rental, a silver Tahoe. She tossed her ruck into the rear compartment, lifted Lucy's bag beside it, and opened the hard-sided rollerboard. Lucy shook her head at the way TK visibly relaxed when she saw the secured firearms box and the two Beretta 9mm semiautomatic pistols nestled in their foam housing. One of the few perks of being a retired federal agent—Lucy could carry her weapons across state lines.

"I thought we agreed to divide and conquer," Lucy said, before TK could reach for her Beretta. "If you're starting with Warren, he won't like you carrying."

"I'm legal in Tennessee," she protested.

"He's now a lieutenant in charge of their SWAT team. I sincerely doubt he'll want a civilian he never met before riding with him with a weapon."

"And you say I'm paranoid." TK looked on with envy as Lucy holstered her own weapon before shutting the case, locking TK's in place.

"Don't worry," Lucy assured her, once they were in the SUV and headed toward the interstate. "As soon as you're done with the sheriff's department, you can have it back."

"Maybe I should go with you? The info Wash dug up on the trailer park guy made him sound kinda sketchy." Arrests for drug possession and facilitating prostitution definitely qualified as "sketchy" in Lucy's mind—one of the reasons Yates was on her list, not TK's.

"I'll be fine." They settled in for the two-hour drive north to Craven County. McCabe called twice, asking for updates, and TK entertained Lucy with fun facts about the area. Craven was the only county in Tennessee that bordered both North Carolina and Georgia. It was almost five hundred square miles but had less than ten thousand people. The Nantahala National Forest occupied more than half of its acreage.

"Imagine being a deputy patrolling that kind of territory," TK said. "I mean, you get called to a domestic out in the middle of the woods, where's your back up? Could be fifty miles away or more."

"You're from West Virginia. Same situation there. Just like parts of Pennsylvania." Including where Lucy had grown up.

"I'm from a *city* in West Virginia. Weirton has twice as many people as the entire Craven County."

"Not sure twenty thousand makes a city."

"Still, it's a proper town with a government and law enforcement and everything. From what McCabe said, sounds like Craven is more like the wild west. Judges making up their own rules, kids getting locked up without a lawyer. Did you read the article Wash found about the feds stepping in after kids were being held for indefinite lengths of time and then had to pay for it, even if no charges were brought?"

"That was a different county."

"Just saying, sounds like Craven is even worse."

Lucy set the cruise control and leaned back. "You don't just want to find Cherish. You want to prove her innocent."

"Don't you? I mean, not necessarily find her innocent, but find the truth? She's the same age as Megan. How would you feel if Megan got locked up like that, practically tried and convicted without even having the chance to talk to you or a lawyer?"

"But Cherish did talk. She confessed, remember?"

"C'mon. You read those transcripts. She was interviewed how many times? And her story kept changing. It was never the same twice."

"Jack Kutler's story never changed." Lucy wasn't even sure why they were having this argument. She was just as suspicious as TK was about what had really happened eleven years ago. But that wasn't the point. "It's not our job to re-open the case. It's our job to learn enough about Cherish to find her now."

TK propped her feet up on the dash, chin down, assuming the same posture Megan did when she disagreed with Lucy. "Yeah. Great job. Find her so they can arrest her all over again."

"We don't know that. The DA might decline to bring charges again."

"In a high profile murder case? I doubt it."

Lucy knew she was probably right. "If we happen to stumble across something that helps clarify Cherish's innocence or guilt, then of course we'll pass it on to McCabe to help her defense. But our main focus is learning about her. Is she tech-savvy enough that she could build a whole new life? Get a fake ID? If so, what kind of job skills does she have? Or would she stay under the radar, maybe live on the street, go dark, no ID, no documented job, no online profile? Is there anyone she might have remained in contact with or who might have helped her?"

"I know the drill. So did the US Marshals and State Police," TK reminded her.

"Which is why we'll focus on talking to the people they ignored in the heat of a manhunt." They'd already decided that TK would concentrate on the people Cherish came in contact with after the shooting—the deputy who arrested her and was first on scene, the detention center staff, and the lawyers who'd played hot potato with Cherish's case, constantly handing it off as proceedings dragged on. Lucy would work the fringes of Cherish's family life— people at the trailer park where she and her grandmother had lived, anyone who'd gone to school or church with her, friends of her mother and grandmother.

She'd been surprised by how many were still living in Craven County—apparently it was the kind of place that was hard to escape from even if you were a fugitive on the run.

CHAPTER 14

THEY LEFT THE INTERSTATE and drove east into the foothills, past the last town large enough to earn a mark on the map, a place named Cleveland, and then kept going into more rugged mountain territory, punctuated by picturesque river valleys and the occasional plateau. It reminded TK a lot of her home in West Virginia.

Finally they reached the outer boundary of Craven County and then Hartfield, the small town that was its county seat. Hartfield sat in a river valley, its buildings hugging the side of a mountain on one side of the water and extending up a series of more gradual hills on the other. The sheriff's station was comparatively newer than the buildings clustered on the other side of the river, with a utilitarian stucco construction that had a seventies sensibility clinging to it. Along with the other government offices it sat midway up the hillside, giving TK a nice view back to downtown. Across the river, the domed courthouse rose still higher, positioned above the rest of Hartfield, higher than even the church steeples.

Lucy dropped her off, but before TK could enter the building, a middle-aged man wearing a khaki lieutenant's uniform came barreling out. Had to be Warren.

"You O'Connor?" he barked, striding toward a patrol car without waiting for her answer.

TK followed but almost ran into him when he abruptly stopped and whirled to face her, one hand jiggling a set of keys, the other resting on the butt of his service weapon. She was close enough to read his nametag. Yep, it was Warren.

"You think you're going to find Cherish Walker after all these years?" Translation: when he and his buddies couldn't. "What makes you think she's even still alive? And if she is, how the hell is seeing an old slaughterhouse going to help find her?"

TK squared her posture, facing him, hands casually held above her waist, mirroring his own not-quite-fighting stance. With a guy like this, you didn't back down or show any weakness. "What can you tell me about that night?"

His gaze lasered up and down her body. "You serve?"

"Marines. Iraq and Afghanistan." Enough to satisfy his curiosity without distracting him with too many details he had no business knowing.

His lips twisted in consideration, and finally he nodded. "I can tell you a lot about that night. No idea what's true or not, though."

"So you don't believe either Jack's or Cherish's account?"

"I believe the evidence. And the only evidence we had that was clear and irrefutable was one dead body and one shot boy."

"Could you walk me through it? You were first on scene, right?"

"Kutler said it was all right, so yeah. You'll have to ride in the back, though. County policy." He dangled the keys to his police cruiser. TK nodded, and Warren opened the rear door and waited for her to slide inside. There were bars on the windows and the seat was a single molded piece of plastic, imbued with the reek of fear, piss, and vomit. She ignored the olfactory overload and sat down, fastening her shoulder harness. The car rocked as he slammed the door. A thick plastic barrier separated her from the driver's compartment, but it had ventilation holes so she could hear Warren's travelogue as he drove.

First, they eased up the road from the sheriff's station and past a complex of three large brick buildings with a parking lot and cluster of bright yellow school buses in front of them. "Used to have another elementary school other side of the valley, but it closed a few years ago. Just about all the kids need bused, so makes more sense having all the schools together anyway."

"Cherish was riding her bike home from school that day."

"Her grandmother had high blood pressure. Didn't take her medicine and had a stroke a few days before. Doctors thought she was doing better, might even get sent home, but then all this business with Cherish, she ended up dying two weeks later. For the best, I guess. She was a proud woman; this would have broken her for sure."

Sounded like despite his earlier protests, he'd long ago made up his mind who was responsible for the shootings that night. "There was a storm that day?"

"Came in around noon." He steered them up a steep set of switchbacks. "That time of year, they come up from the Gulf. Tropical storms and hurricanes. Outer bands and the winds are the hammer while the mountains act like an anvil with us caught between. Say another one's headed this way in a day or two—Delilah's her name. But the one back then didn't have a name, not that I can recall."

He slowed down for a sharp curve, mottled sunlight streaming through the thick trees the only sign of the sky above. "Right about here is where Cherish said her bike went off the road. Who knows for sure? After the storm we couldn't find any evidence."

"She said the Kutler boys ran her off the road in their truck."

"Said a lot of things. Never the same thing twice. She skidded on the wet pavement, lost control. Hank stopped to help. She was riding and the boys and their truck came up behind her, scared her, and she crashed. She didn't see them at all until it was too late, and when she tried to get out of their way, she ran off the road. They saw her and aimed right for her, forcing her off the road. Take your pick."

"Jack said she'd already wrecked when they drove past, saw her, and stopped to help."

"Makes more sense than anything she told us. Because why would she get in that truck with two boys and let them take her anywhere if they'd forced her off the road?"

The trees were old and tall, crowding the narrow road. TK imagined riding a bike up the steep grade, wind slamming into you, rain blinding you, unable to hear or see anything, wet and miserable and cold, just wanting to get home. "She might not have realized at first that they ran her off the road. And she'd known them all her life—"

"Everyone knew the Kutlers. They was good boys. Were going to make it out of here, make something of themselves. Even after everything, Jack still did. Works for his stepdad's investment firm up in Nashville."

"So Cherish would have trusted them. At least at first."

"No reason not to trust them boys. Good church-going family, the Kutlers." *Unlike the Walkers*, his tone implied.

They crested the top of the mountain. Or maybe foothill was a better term, TK thought, as she gazed past the plateau to the majesty of the Appalachians rising up to the east.

"Used to be some of the best farm land around. But look at it now." Warren made a snorting noise. "Gated vacation communities where the houses cost more than anyone who actually lives here makes in ten years of working to the bone. Just stand empty most of the year—especially after the recession. A lot of them were foreclosed—we'd get transients stripping their wires and ransacking them, others just squatting. Million-dollar houses and junkies crashing there, calling them home. Some even tried to claim squatter's rights."

She noted how he made it sound as if all the problems came from the outside world, with the residents of Craven County playing the role of angelic host. He met her gaze in the rearview mirror and scowled as if he knew what she was thinking. "We got our own troubles, that's for sure. But nothing like we seen once folks discovered Craven and began building their McMansions, bringing us false hope that folks here would have jobs again and a chance at their own dreams."

They passed through a thickly wooded section and hit the far end of the small plateau, the mountains towering over them. "This used to all be Kutler land. Cattle grazing to the west, back the way we came, and they had their homestead over there," he gestured at a drive leading into the woods, its pavement broken and littered with potholes, "and the slaughterhouse back here where it's steep. Nowhere for a stray cow to run to, not the way the limestone shears up and the forest gets so thick."

They emerged from the trees, and TK saw what he meant. In the clearing at the base of the mountain stood a building that had to be the slaughterhouse. It was constructed of cement block covered by a tin roof; its length was out of proportion to its height, making it seem weirdly off balance. Surrounding it was a rusted metal fence topped with barbed wire. Along one side, the fence created a path—the same way they corralled tourists at Disney—leading to a large sliding door. The oppressive atmosphere was compounded by the way the mountain jutted up as if it had been thrust out of the ground, so steep that the trees crowding its lower slopes grew at an unnatural angle, not quite horizontal, barely hanging on by their roots.

"It happened in the office," Warren said, pointing to a squat square addition at the near end of the building. He climbed out of the car and sauntered around to release TK from the backseat. Once free, she gulped in the mountain air, tasting pine.

"Why would they drive past their home to bring Cherish here?" TK asked. "This place was already shut down by then, right?"

"Jack said his parents didn't approve of the Walkers, and he and Hank didn't want to get in trouble. And they had tools to fix her bike here."

She thought of the crime scene photos. "But they never even took the bike out of the truck. That makes no sense."

"Whole thing makes no sense. All I know is by the end of the night, we have two boys shot and one girl, not a scratch on her, with her prints on the weapon."

"The boys' prints were on it as well."

"Of course. It was their gun." He led her through a gate to the office door, which he unlocked with a key dangling from a ring.

"I'm surprised they didn't sell it," TK said, as they crossed the threshold into a dank, dark, windowless room that was only about twelve feet deep, but because it ran the width of the barn it was attached to, was at least twice that in length. "Or tear it down."

Warren clicked on the lights. "Mrs. Kutler wanted to, but the old man said it was Jack's legacy, so it was up to him. Jack said he couldn't bear to part with all the memories of the good times he and Hank had here."

The rear wall of the room was lined with file cabinets, and there was a splintered desk pushed against the wall. A tumbled stack of CDs sat beside an old-style boom box. In the center of the floor was a battered coffee table with old bench car seats on either side. The cinderblock walls held the mildewed, curled up remnants of posters—scantily clad girls posing with guns, *Sports Illustrated* swimsuit models, more girls from the old Carl's Jr. ads, licking hamburger grease from their fingers. Every wall was peppered with holes. *Target practice*, TK thought, as she ran her finger along the crumbled edge of one and uncovered a bullet buried inside the wall. She hoped the boys had been smart enough to wear ear protection—it would be deafening shooting in this enclosed environment. Some of the posters had been used as targets, but either wall at each end of the long room also had scattered holes roughly where a man's head would stand.

For a slaughterhouse, it didn't smell of meat—rather, it smelled like ammonia and bleach. Guess that made sense; you'd need to keep the place as clean as possible to pass health inspections. She stopped, staring at the drain in the center of the floor.

"Whole place is built like that," Warren said. "So you can hose it all down and clear it of any contamination."

She glanced up from the drain to the solid metal door at the rear of the room. "That leads into the actual killing floor?"

"Yep. No one's been back there for years." He pulled the key ring back out and selected one. "Want to see?"

"No, thanks." The kids had never gone

back there, so there was no reason she should—even if she were inclined to visit a slaughterhouse. "Mr. Kutler still lives here?"

"No. Once his wife left him and took Jack, he moved down to Florida. Said this was Jack's place now to do with what he liked."

"Jack comes back here?"

"Sure. Football games, holidays, I'll see him around. Never know when he'll stop by to pay his respects at Hank's grave. Sometimes he'll stand a round in Hank's name at the Lucky Penny—just show up for a day or two and vanish again." He shook his head. "Kinda surprising, you ask me. I were him, I'm not sure I'd ever come back here."

TK had the feeling Warren wasn't just talking about the slaughterhouse and the scene of the crime.

CHAPTER 15

AFTER SHE DROPPED TK at the Craven County sheriff's station for her meeting with Lieutenant Warren, Lucy drove east into the foothills to the trailer court Cherish had once called home.

She'd spoken to the manager yesterday—his name was Yates, and on the phone his accent had been so thick she'd imagined him as overweight with a thick beard that muffled his words. Instead, when she approached the doublewide labeled OFFICE, where she'd found him waiting for her on the deck, a small fan plugged into an extension cord and propped up on a beer cooler, aiming a stream of air into his clean-shaven face, she found he wasn't fat at all, rather the kind of skinny that no amount of eating could pad, with high cheekbones and a dark complexion that spoke of part Cherokee heritage.

"Mr. Yates? I'm Lucy Guardino. We spoke yesterday."

He raised a chipped porcelain mug and spat a steam of tobacco into it. "You want to know about the Walkers. Tessa and her girl and granddaughter."

Although he made no move to invite her to join him, Lucy pulled the other folding canvas chair close and sat down. "Yes. I'm interested in anyone who knew Cherish Walker."

"So you said. But you're not a cop." His tone was laced with suspicion.

"No, sir. Have you seen Cherish? Has she ever returned?"

"Not if she knows what's good for her. Not after what she did to those Kutler boys." He spat again, but this time it was less about reducing the load of tobacco juice between his cheek and gums and more about punctuating his feelings about Cherish. "No one around here is forgetting that, not anytime soon."

"Cherish lived here with her grandmother for over two years. Maybe she snuck back to take something of her old life with her?" Lucy wasn't hopeful; she simply wanted to get him talking.

He snorted. "Wouldn't have had anything to take. What I didn't sell, I burned. Long before she ran off."

"Excuse me?"

"Perfectly within my rights. First of the month came along and no rent, so I padlocked the place. Two weeks later, the grandmother died. Lease was in her name, so I confiscated their possessions. Not like the girl was ever coming back again—she was either going to prison or foster care. Cleaned out the place and had it rented again by the end of the month."

"Did you keep anything? Anything I could see?"

"Nope." He aimed another stream of tobacco juice into the mug. "I'm a business man, ain't nothing personal. I liked Tessa, the grandmother. She weren't at all like Cherry or her mother. Those Walker girls, they was wild. No surprise they ended up the way they did."

"You knew Cherish's mother?"

"Sure. Tessa had her trailer here ever since they sold off the last of the family land back in '78 or thereabouts. Her old man worked one of the last copper mines—those boys all died young. Toxic fumes or some such. Tessa, she had no choice in the matter, not with all the money they owed. Had to sell up and go begging for any job she could get. But that girl of hers, would she take charity? Not from the likes of me." He hitched up his T-shirt, revealing a straight-edged scar running along the side of his belly. "That's how a Walker girl repays you when you offer them charity. Come to think on it, she did this here when she was about the same age as Cherry when Cherry shot them Kutler boys."

"Cherish's mother stabbed you? Was she arrested?"

His laugh seemed more nervous than amused as he looked down and tucked his shirt back in. "I ain't the kind of man calls the police for every little squabble. Barely needed any stitching."

"Exactly what kind of charity did you offer her?" Lucy was careful to keep her tone neutral.

"Nothing for her to get so riled up about. Just a chance to make a little money—help her mom out, put food on the table, keep a roof over their head." His shoulders straightened in righteous indignation. "And look what happened to her daughter. Them Kutler boys trying to help her out after she wrecked her bike, and as soon as she gets her hands on a gun, she shoots them for their trouble."

The way he described the crime, it made Cherish seem either psychotic or...a desperate victim fighting for her life. "Why exactly would Cherish do that, do you think?"

He stared at her like she was an idiot. "Why? The Kutlers were rich. She wanted their money, of course. Her mother died same way, double-dealing her man. I'm telling you, those Walker women, they hate men—never turn your back on a Walker girl."

"Her mother's dead?" Lucy asked. "We

couldn't find any record of her." At least not since she'd been admitted to the burn center in Chattanooga when Cherish was twelve.

"Oh, yeah, she's sure as certain dead. Boyfriend was one of those Reapers—motorcycle gang used to run up and down these mountains before the feds busted them. Anyway, they robbed a liquor store over in Chattanooga. Got away with a few hundred and all the booze they could carry." He leaned forward, close enough that Lucy could smell the rancid tobacco wafting from his mouth. "Out in the parking lot, they start arguing over a bottle of whiskey. She wants it, he won't let her have it, she stabs him—just like she did me—her boyfriend shoots her dead, hightails out of there, cops on his heels, and she's lying dead in the mud. Buried her as a Jane Doe. Boyfriend made it out okay— rented a place to him and his new woman a few months later."

"When was this? Did Cherish know her mother had died?"

"Month or two after Cherry shot the Kutler boys. I mean, that's when I found out. Doubt anyone would have bothered to track down a next of kin, not when they didn't even bother to find out her real name. Besides, she'd already given up on Cherry years before. You know how Cherry got those scars on her arms, don't ya?"

"She was burned in a fire when she was twelve."

He made a scoffing noise, coupling it with another spitful of tobacco juice. "Cabin her pa built for them, before he went off to war and got himself killed. After that, her ma was useless. Just fell apart. Couldn't work, couldn't even get herself dressed most days. Lost her job. Doctor gave her pills, then more pills, then she began to drink, and then she found herself a new way to forget her pain—meth. The Reapers ran the meth trade, and she hooked up with them. Ended up burning down her own cabin. Cherry wasn't in the cabin, but she ran back and pulled her ma out of the fire."

"Pretty brave for a kid."

"Saved her ma, sure. But left two men inside to burn alive. I heard tell she bolted them in, no way out. Fact is, I'll bet she started the fire herself. I'm telling you, those Walker women..." He shook his head as if he'd run out of words to describe the man-hating, murderous Walker women.

"That's when Cherish moved in with her grandmother. Here."

"Yep. I let the girl come—but no way in hell was I letting her ma anywhere near. Guess she wasn't too interested—took off with the Reapers straight from the graveyard after they buried their buddies. Rode off on the back of one of their bikes and never looked back."

CHAPTER 16

MOST OF THAT FIRST DAY I was at the detention
center, they kept me locked in that same
windowless room. *Isolation*, they called it.
Observation. For my own good. Until they were
certain I was "stable."

They said it was so they could do "wellness
checks." Which translated to waking me as soon
as I fell asleep. By that afternoon I was so
disoriented, hung over, sleep deprived, and
terrified that I would have confessed to
anything. If the cops had returned or anyone
asked.

They didn't.

It was just me and four blank walls and my

own nightmare memories of what had happened at the slaughterhouse. No one would tell me how Jack was—if he was even still alive—and no one let me call my gran, though they said she'd taken a turn and couldn't talk, so now I was worried she was dead or dying from the shock of hearing what had happened. All I could think about was that it was all my fault. If I hadn't gotten into that truck, gone with Hank and Jack, grabbed for the gun...

I sat on the bunk, rubbing at the burn scars on my arms—the skin there doesn't feel like normal skin when it's touched, it tingles with tiny lightning strikes of electricity. The doctors said that was a good sign, meant the nerves were still alive, just damaged. Took me months to get used to it enough to sleep through the night—every time I moved, the air would hit or the pillow or the sheets and I'd jerk awake with the shock. Now, though, it's kind of comforting, a pain that I control. Makes me feel less numb. Reminds me I'm alive.

Finally, the detention center staff decided I was "stable" enough to be let out for dinner.

One of the staff, a woman not much older than me, showed me to the commons room where the other kids—she called them *residents*—hung out between their classes—yeah, we still had school, a teacher came in every day—and work duties. There were fake leather couches with duct tape covering holes in the upholstery; a bunch of plastic patio chairs; a few tables where kids sat working puzzles, drawing, and doing homework; and one TV bolted to the wall behind a scratched Plexiglas cover that made the picture look frizzled.

The other kids drew most of my attention. There were guys and girls. They pretty much all looked older than me except for one guy who was maybe my age. They were black and white—a few more white kids, but that made sense since Craven County was mostly white. The boys outnumbered the girls; no surprise there, I guess. But the girls seemed harder, with their deadeye stares and tight lips. The boys were relaxed, like this was some kind of summer camp. The girls—they were sharp, focused like when you're hunting and the deer senses danger, the way it looks before it bolts, every sense on fire.

I've been around mean girls before at school, mostly just kept out of their way and stayed off their radar, but now I realized those girls were Barbie dolls compared to these girls. And I was definitely on their radar, their glares lasers targeting me.

"Who's the newbie?" one of the white girls called out from her seat on the couch where a black girl was braiding her hair. She was like a queen, holding court. Queen of the vampires, I thought, from the way her smile bared her teeth until the points of her incisors rested on her red, red lips.

"Folks, this is Cherish. I expect you to treat her with respect and show her the ropes," the counselor said. "Dinner in ten."

The counselor left me standing there, now the center of their attention. The only person who didn't seem to care about me was another staff member, sitting on a chair in the far corner. He barely glanced up from his phone, and when he did it was to acknowledge his colleague, not me.

The white girl stood. She had long blonde hair twisted into an intricate pattern of teeny-tiny braids that must have taken forever. The black girl stood up beside her—she was shorter and younger than the blonde but looked ready to fight. Then another white girl joined them. I took a step back; not sure why. It was as if an invisible fist had punched me from across the room. They hated me, and I had no idea why.

"I'm Brenda," the blonde said. "Let me show you around, Cherry." She used the nickname I hated, the one the kids at school used. I was a freshman, had only been at the high school for a little over a month, but I couldn't remember seeing her. How did she know me?

Before I could protest, she sidled up to me, taking my arm in hers as if we were best friends. The other two girls followed close behind us, pressing their bodies against mine, herding me. A few of the boys glanced up, and one laughed before plopping onto the couch Brenda had just vacated. His laugh reminded me of Jack's, and I shivered.

"This is the rec area, that door leads into the dining hall, over there is the gym, and there's the class room—oh, Cherry, you'll love our library. People from all the churches donate all sorts of books to help us see the light and rehabilitate." Brenda's voice turned sing-song, as if she were preaching. The other girls giggled, and one of them pinched my butt so hard I jumped. "Mr. Richard, we can show Cherry the library, right? It won't take long, I promise."

The counselor waved his hand, granting permission, without looking up.

"Thank you, Mr. Richard." Brenda's voice dripped with sugar. She opened the door to the library and held it for us as the other two girls shoved me inside.

It wasn't a large room—about the same size as my cell but without a sink and toilet. The walls were floor to ceiling lined with shelves, and the shelves were filled with books. In the center of the room was a reading table surrounded by chairs. I would have loved this room. If I wasn't busy getting punched in the kidney.

The first blow took me by surprise—not the punch as much as how well positioned it was and the sudden flash of pain. As I turned, someone kicked my leg out from under me, and just like that I was on the floor, gasping to breathe. One girl yanked my hair so hard I felt strands rip free of my scalp while the other kept her knee in my back like a fulcrum, ready to break my spine if I tried to resist.

Brenda scooted a chair to sit above my face. She twirled a rusted nail about two inches long in her delicate, long, princess-vampire fingers. "We heard about Jack and Hank. Jack says you're trying to make it all Hank's fault."

I gasped—not from pain but from relief. Jack was alive, and well enough to talk!

She leaned down, tracing the nail from my lips up to my eye. "There must be two dozen Bibles in this library, maybe more. The church folks all think everything we need is in the Good Book. Maybe it is." The nail was now pressed right below my eye, so hard that tears were leaking out. "Ever hear of an eye for an eye,

Cherry?"

One of the girls behind me snickered while the second one, the one holding my hair, wrapped her free arm around my throat, choking me.

"You're going to tell the cops you were drunk and high and stupid, and that whatever you told them last night was a lie. You're going to tell them the truth—that it was all your fault. You freaked out. You grabbed the gun and shot Jack and Hank. They didn't do anything wrong. It was all you, Cherry. Stupid little you. You're only fourteen, they'll blame it on the Molly and let you go."

Molly? That was ecstasy—no wonder I'd felt so strange. *They'd drugged me? Why? Stupid, Cherish, you know why. Stupid, stupid, stupid.*

Brenda sensed my attention drift. She poked the nail into my eye—I blinked and it hit my eyelid, but it still hurt. The pressure on my back eased as her friend swung around and pried my eyelids open. Brenda's face filled my vision. The nail was so close I couldn't even focus on it, but I felt it with each heart beat, so close it was almost touching my eyeball.

"Maybe you're the kind of girl we can't trust to do the right thing. Maybe we need to show you a lesson first? Let you feel half the pain that Jack is feeling right now?" She pressed the nail even closer. I held my breath, held my entire body as still as possible. Pain shot through my eye as the tip of the nail scratched it. I couldn't scream, not without the girl's arm tight around my throat.

Then she eased back the tiniest bit. "No. I think we can give you one last chance. Right, Cherry? You're going to tell the cops the truth. It was all you. All your fault. All your stupid little schoolgirl crush—taking drugs, thinking it would make Hank and Jack like you, notice your pathetic skinny ass. Jack and Hank had nothing to do with it, right?"

She paused, the nail hovering an inch away. Far enough that I could safely nod my head.

Brenda flounced to her feet and touched her hair, hiding the nail in her braids. "All right, then. Let's go. Can't be late for dinner, right? Today's mac and cheese. Yummo."

The other two girls hauled me up. I was doubled over, not sure if I was going to vomit from the pain in my eye or my back or my head. The eye was the worst, the light stabbing at it like a cattle prod. We stumbled back out to the commons area.

"Mr. Richard?" Brenda was saying. "I think maybe Cherry's still hung over or high or something? She says she might puke, that she doesn't feel too well."

He rolled his eyes and looked up at me where I was swaying and blinking hard, clutching my belly with one hand and my eye with the other. "All right, then. Back to isolation."

And that was it. Without my saying a word, my fate was now sealed.

CHAPTER 17

FOR THE NEXT FEW HOURS, Lucy spent more time driving to each of her interviews than any of the actual discussions lasted. The consensus was virtually unanimous: Cherish Walker was quiet, never made any trouble until she shot the Kutler boys; but given her mother, no one was surprised that she'd turned out the way she had.

Still, Lucy managed to ferret out a few details that weren't in any of the case files. Cherish's junior high school teacher said she had a flare for design and often drew intricate graphics. "Real pretty flowers and vines and paisley-like curves. Then she started drawing them on herself—to cover up those nasty burn scars. Of course, that's against school policy, so I called her grandmother, and Cherish had to wear long sleeves until the marker had faded away. That's the only time I remember anyone here ever needing to discipline her at all. She was such a quiet girl—just sat in the back and never called attention to herself."

A man who had grown up with Cherish's father and served in the Army with him told Lucy, "I tried to keep an eye on them when I got home—it was hard, because I was messed up myself and then Sally was expecting our first. Cherish was living with her granny by then, but I went and took her hunting a few times. So much like her dad. Quiet, but in a good way, not daydreaming but always watching, you know what I mean? She could move through the wood like a spring breeze, without disturbing the game. Had a good eye—her daddy taught her well. You know what, even though she was a girl, I think she liked it better in the woods than being around people. She just seemed more relaxed. Or maybe that was me—back then I definitely preferred my own company most days, at least until I got myself sorted out. I was real sorry to hear what she did to those Kutler boys. But after living with her mom—well, living with that woman, going to war might have been easier, know what I mean?"

No one Lucy spoke with questioned Cherish's guilt—either they trusted their legal system that much (which she doubted) or they admired the Kutler family too much to imagine the shooting could have happened any other way. "Besides, she confessed," was a recurring theme along with lurid suggestions of "the goings-on" of Cherish's mother after her husband went to war.

By the time she reached her final subject— the wife of Cherish's old minister—Lucy had two competing profiles for Cherish. The one that appeared in all the case files echoed so many descriptions of mass shooters: quiet, kept to herself, but no one surprised when the smoldering volcano finally erupted into violence. But there was also another, more nuanced glimpse of the girl Cherish could have been:

smart, quick-thinking, independent, self-sufficient, artistic, observant.

These new insights didn't give her any hint as to Cherish's innocence or guilt, but they did paint a totally different picture of the kind of fugitive she might have been. The police had focused on major transportation hubs leading from the county seat—particularly Route 74, which led to the Interstate. They'd scoured CCTV searching for a fugitive hopping onto a bus or hitchhiking, put out flyers and alerts along I-75 and the other major roadways, and sent email blasts to all the hostels, hotels, motels, homeless shelters, churches, and other agencies who might notice a lone teen living on the street. The nearest cities were Chattanooga and Atlanta, so they'd concentrated their efforts to the west and south of Craven County.

And came up empty.

Lucy thought about how Megan had accused her of bias, that if the genders had been reversed and it had been a teenaged boy accused of assaulting two girls, she'd be thinking of Cherish as a predator rather than a victim. It wasn't true—well, maybe it was, simply because that was her first instinct after so many years of working these kind of crimes. But Lucy had learned early in her career to never assume anything, not even who was truly the victim and who was the perpetrator.

Maybe that was why she had a feeling she knew exactly how Cherish had escaped. She needed to go to the courthouse—the last place Cherish had been seen—to test her theory.

If the minister's wife, Helen Overkamp, hadn't been on Lucy's way to the courthouse, Lucy might have skipped their appointment. Instead, she pulled up to a small whitewashed frame building with a large cross above the door and hurried in, anxious to finish and get to the courthouse. She finally felt like she had a handle on this case.

Once inside, she was surprised to find a reception area filled with sick people. She did a double take and glanced at the sign over the door. ALL SOULS MINISTRY, it read. But below it, in a different font, had been added: *WALK-IN CLINIC*. She wove her way past a woman with a leg swollen like an elephant's, a young man wracked with coughing spasms so violent they bent him double, an older man clenching a bloody bandanna to his arm, and a young pregnant woman bouncing a toddler on her knee while another slightly older child played at her feet.

"I'm here to see Helen Overkamp," Lucy told the elderly woman sitting behind the receptionist desk. "Lucy Guardino."

The woman jerked her head up to assess Lucy, performing some kind of mental triage. She folded her arms across her chest and shook her head as if Lucy had been judged unworthy. "She's busy." Her tone implied that Lucy was a cretin to not have already figured that out for herself. "Try again tomorrow."

"We had an appointment."

"Not today you don't. Today's walk-ins only."

"Which I just did."

"You don't look sick. What's wrong with you?"

"I'm not sick. I need to speak to Ms.

Overkamp. If you could just let her know I'm here—"

The woman ended the argument by simply lowering her head to return working on her crossword puzzle, as if Lucy's existence were no longer was worthy of acknowledgement. Lucy debated between leaving—she wanted to check out the courthouse before they closed for the day—arguing, waiting, or simply barging past the old woman and finding Overkamp herself. Which, given the sour expressions on the others favored her with, might cause a small riot.

Luckily the door behind the reception desk opened and an overweight woman emerged, carrying a slip of paper clutched in her hand. Behind her was another woman in her late fifties wearing a white lab coat and stethoscope. She glanced at Lucy and blinked in surprise.

"Says you made an appointment," the receptionist said, her tone one of rebuke.

"Right. Sorry. I forgot to tell you."

"Can't do much good if you don't."

"I'm sorry, Gloria."

From the receptionist's expression, Lucy

had the feeling the discussion was one frequently repeated. She stepped into the fray. "Helen Overkamp? I'm Lucy Guardino. We spoke on the phone last night?"

Overkamp looked past Lucy to scour the waiting room with her gaze, and then glanced at the clipboard on the receptionist's desk. "George, why don't you come back and we'll get that wound soaking while I speak with this lady."

The receptionist sighed and glared at Lucy before smiling at the man with the bandage and leading him past her back into the rear of the building. Overkamp and Lucy followed behind.

"I thought this was a church," Lucy said, as they passed several examination rooms and ended up in a small office area.

Overkamp closed the door and took a seat behind a desk. There were photos of her and a man in a clerical collar—her husband, Lucy presumed—along with several framed diplomas. Doctor of Divinity in the name of Martin Overkamp along with a Bachelor's of Nursing Science and a nurse practitioner's degree in the name of Helen Overkamp.

"Sit, please." Overkamp waved a hand to the chair opposite her desk. "This was a church—my husband's dream. We spent every penny buying this place after we were married, tending to our congregation."

"Spiritually and medically?"

"Exactly. Only the clinic wasn't here, of course. Not back then. I used to work with the local family physician. But he died, and then Martin died and here I was, no job, no husband, spiritually bereft. But with the closest doctor now all the way over in Cleveland, people just kept wandering in, knocking on my door, and asking for help. And I realized, as always, that the good Lord had provided a solution for me and our congregation." She smiled, her gaze going to a photo of her husband. Then she shook herself and returned her attention to Lucy. "But that's not what you came to discuss. You asked about Cherish Walker."

"I know her grandmother, Tessa, attended your husband's church, so I hoped you might have some insights." It was a long shot.

"Tessa. What a special soul. So generous and patient. I'm afraid I can't tell you much about Cherish, though. Such a quiet girl. Guarded. It wasn't easy to earn her trust. She definitely had her doubts about religion—Martin and Tessa despaired of her ever being baptized. But I think, maybe in part because of our discussions after she was incarcerated, at least I hope, she changed her mind and finally found her faith."

Lucy stilled. "Excuse me—you had contact with Cherish after she was arrested?"

Overkamp nodded. "I was the nurse for the detention center. Unfortunately, Cherish ended up seeing me quite often. It was almost as if she was punishing herself—or preparing herself, I'm not sure. The children targeted her, and the adults turned their backs and didn't protect her. Even though she was quite capable, Cherish refused to ever fight back. Of course, things got worse after Sylva left."

Lucy held her breath. None of this was in the case files—only a few photos documenting injuries Cherish sustained, but no personal insights. "Sylva?"

"Sylva Wright. Another girl detained there. A few years older than Cherish, but she quite literally saved Cherish's life. You have to understand—the other children, they all knew the Kutlers, they knew what Cherish had done. Or was accused of doing. Locked up in such close quarters, she was just as much their prisoner as she was the county's." She paused, her gaze distant. "I hate to judge; they were only children caught in difficult circumstances. But all that wrath focused on one small girl... They would have killed Cherish, I'm certain. If not for Sylva."

CHAPTER 18

ONCE THEY RELEASED ME FROM ISOLATION, the next few days passed in a whirlwind. Meetings with my probation officer, my caseworker, the detention center's doctor, an orientation session with the staff, and a mental health evaluation, which translated to filling in little bubbles on a test with questions like "Do you generally consider yourself a happy person?"

Most important, though I didn't know it at the time, was my first meeting with my new roommate: Sylva. She was a thin black girl, seventeen, arrested for assault after hitting her mother's boyfriend with a lamp. He'd been trying to rape her—she said—but both her mother and the man said it was unprovoked, so here she sat until her eighteenth birthday when she'd be released with no home and no family, thrown into the deep end of her life to sink or swim.

Sylva. I wish I'd paid more attention to the moment when I first saw her, before she saw me. The cell was the last one at the end of the building, and because of a utility closet beside it, was shorter and wider than the other rooms. It had two narrow cots, but they were situated not across from each other but at ninety degrees along the far corner, their heads placed together, just a few inches separating them. There was a window high up in the cinderblock wall, its glass wire-mesh and unbreakable, like all the windows here. The sunlight refracted strangely through the thick glass, separating into soft ribbons that cascaded down to where Sylva lay on her bunk reading a book. Even then she was fiercely determined not to waste a moment. If the courts said she had to be locked up for two and a half years, then by God, she was going to make the best of it, and use the time to prepare herself for what came next.

Her gaze lifted from the words on the page to me. I stopped, clutching the stack of linens I'd been given, not sure if I needed to ask permission to enter the space that was to become my home. She was beautiful. But not pretty. Not with her reedy-thin arms and sharp cheekbones. Sylva's beauty never had anything to do with what you saw when you looked at her; it was more about how she saw you.

What did Sylva see with her first glance of me? Not much except a terrified girl barely holding it together, on the brink of collapse. As I stood, wavering, she moved with certain purpose. She closed her book with a bookmark, setting it aside on her bunk, stood up in one fluid movement, and somehow crossed the space between us before I could take another breath. She ignored me to focus on the staff nurse, Helen, who'd escorted me out of Isolation.

"Take this guppy back," Sylva told Helen. "She's too little to be swimming down here in the deep water. Ain't you got room in the kiddie pool?"

Later I learned she meant sending me to a group foster home instead of keeping me locked up with the "hardened" offenders.

"Can't. She's charged with a felony." Helen paused. "A violent felony. One with possible repercussions." She stressed the last word.

"What sort of repercussions?" Sylva asked, eyeing me as if taking inventory. She did not seem impressed by what she saw.

"The sort that could cause grievous harm to the balance of our delicate social environment."

My brain gave up trying to interpret their code. Clearly I'd need to learn a new language here. But that thought brought home the fact that I would be staying here for the foreseeable future. My case worker had said that there would be hearings and evaluations, and it might be months before they even knew if I'd have to face being charged as an adult, and if that happened then it would be even longer. He told me Gran's doctors said she was still in serious condition—had developed pneumonia on top of the stroke—and even if she survived, she'd need months of rehab and possibly a nursing home. She'd never be able to take care of me again. One way or the other, I was on my own.

The funny thing was—and I should have asked more questions those first days, but I was shocked numb with exhaustion and fear—no one seemed to even consider the fact that I'd done nothing wrong.

"Looks like the Barbies already had a go at her." Sylva nodded to the bruises that had blossomed around my throat and the gauze patch the nurse had taped over my scratched eyeball.

"Only round one," Helen said.

Sylva and Helen continued their silent staring contest for a moment more while I shifted my burden from one arm to the other, not at all certain what I should do. Finally, they came to an understanding, with Sylva standing aside and waving her arm to usher me into my new home.

I crossed the threshold not sure if I should feel relief at not being turned away or dread because it was clear this was the best I could hope for. I stumbled to my cot and collapsed onto the naked, plastic-coated mattress, hugging my linens to my chest. Maybe if I closed my eyes and held very, very still, this would all go away.

It didn't. When I opened my eyes Sylva was standing over me, hands on her hips, looking much older and wiser than anyone I'd ever met. Even Gran.

"It's not a dream," she said. "Get your ass out of bed, and we'll get you sorted out. Best hurry because it's almost time for dinner and it's cherry cobbler night. I don't care if there's bones sticking out or blood gushing, I don't miss cherry cobbler night for anyone."

As I followed her directions—you'd think I'd never made my own bed before—I felt like I was outside myself, watching. How had this pasty-pale white girl with the stringy brown hair stinking of anti-lice shampoo gotten here? It all felt so surreal, like it was happening to someone else.

Sylva worked with me, her hands correcting mine when I faltered, my mind drifting. I didn't know why I had to take all the blame for what happened—I hadn't done anything wrong except to accept help when the twins accidentally ran me off the road. In fact, now that I'd had time to go over it in my head, I wondered if maybe it hadn't been an accident after all. Maybe Jack had purposefully sped up and steered into me. Maybe I was just the pawn in some sick power game he and his brother had been playing—it sure felt like whatever enjoyment they'd had that night had nothing to do with me and everything to do with each other.

Not that I'd ever be able to explain that weird vibe to anyone. My caseworker hadn't even asked me how I'd ended up with the twins. Guess he took it for granted that I'd wanted to be there, had offered up something to be there. After all, I wasn't exactly homecoming queen material.

We finished making my bed and putting away the new clothes they'd given me: white cotton panties and bras along with beige scrub tops and elastic-waisted pants like what nurses wear. We folded my towels and washcloths and placed them on the shelf beside Sylva's. We filed out when the bell rang for dinner and ate side by side, never saying a word to each other. Some of the other kids tried to talk to me, but Sylva sent them away with a glare. I could tell they were posturing, trying to show the newbie who was boss, but at that point I was too numb to care.

Word of what had happened to Hank and Jack had spread, leading to even more whispers and stares in my direction, none of them friendly. All these kids went to my school; most of them probably knew the twins. And they blamed me—after all, Hank was dead and Jack next to it. Who else was there to blame?

I touched the tape holding my eye patch in place. It was finally setting in that I was in big, big trouble, and the grownups who were supposed to be in charge probably weren't any different from these kids—they'd take the easy way out, avoid a public scandal or smearing the reputation of one of Craven County's oldest and proudest families, and cast me in the role of the bad guy.

After dinner we headed back to our cell—the staff called it a dorm room, but it was really a jail cell, and I had to accept that fact. It wasn't hard—the idea felt familiar. In some ways, I'd been living inside jail cells ever since Dad left. First the cabin, then Gran's trailer, and now here. All the same.

I curled up on my bunk, face to the wall, and covered my eyes with my hands, pushing so hard my vision went red, trying to force away the sight of all that blood. The sounds of gunshots kept screaming through my head as the whole night played itself backwards, forwards, inside out, over and over again.

Finally, it was lights out. I sobbed as quietly as I could, but it wasn't long before I felt Sylva crawl into the bunk behind me, curling her arms and legs around me, holding me tight until I felt her heart beating against my spine.

"Let it all out," she whispered. "You're safe here with me. I won't let anyone hurt you. Not while I'm around."

Words of comfort offered to a scared girl.

Sylva had no idea what that promise would eventually cost her. Or that she'd pay the price with her own blood.

175

Chapter 19

Not that Megan would ever tell Lucy, but she was kind of excited to go back to work at Beacon Falls. Sure, she'd grumbled as Lucy ditched her to leave for Tennessee, and of course she let Valencia treat her to a sumptuous breakfast, but then she dashed upstairs to her office and plunged back into the case.

She spent the morning finishing building her timelines. There were still holes and gaps in logic that made her wonder how either side could have expected to win their case in court.

"If someone's innocent until proven guilty," she asked Valencia over lunch, "then how could they arrest Cherish? Best I can tell, it boils down to her word against Jack Kutler's."

"It's very rare that there is absolute proof of anyone's guilt or innocence. I suspect, with Cherish's grandmother being sick, they arrested her because they were worried about her running away."

"Guess she proved them right." Megan sipped at the chilled soup Valencia had served in a pretty cocktail glass. Lucy never made meals like this, not even when she'd been home recuperating from her leg injury. Then the fridge had been stocked with mail-order protein shakes and supplements to help her heal faster. If it wasn't for Megan's dad actually going to do real shopping, it would probably be months before they had any fresh fruit or vegetables. "What's this called again?"

"Gazpacho. If you have a garden, you can make it yourself. I'll give you the recipe."

"My mom used to garden. She loved it; spent all day out there sometimes." A sigh escaped Megan. "That was last year."

"Your mother suffered a lot of upheaval this year. Your entire family, in fact." Valencia patted Megan's hand, and Megan didn't even flinch or pull away from the touch—not like she did when Lucy tried to do the same thing. Sometimes her mom just made her feel so...prickly.

"Cherish Walker's grandmother died right after they arrested her. She never got to say goodbye or go to the funeral or anything."

Valencia nodded, waiting. Megan liked that about her. She was never in any rush.

"But none of the records say what happened to Cherish's mother. If I was a kid, running away from the cops, I'd go find my mom—wouldn't you? But there's almost nothing about her in the files."

"You think you can find Cherish's mother?"

Megan hesitated. If she were having this discussion with Lucy, this would be where things got tricky. Especially as she was meant to be grounded from electronics. But this was work, right? "I think maybe I already have. Last night, I had an idea, so I went online and looked around. Then this morning—well, I think maybe it's her."

Instead of a barrage of accusations and protests over her extracurricular online sleuthing and the risks posed by using her own computer, Valencia simply nodded again. "I see. And how exactly—"

This was the hard part. "I pretended to be someone else. It's called catfishing—you set up a fake profile, then use it to connect with other people." Valencia looked blank. "On social media? Like SnapChat and Twitter and Facebook?"

"Who did you pretend to be, Megan?"

No way was Megan telling her that—not and risk it getting back to Lucy. "That's not the point. The point is, I figured I'd try Facebook since that's what old people use, and Cherish's mom would be like forty or more, right? And I found someone with her name and birthday."

Valencia pushed back her chair. "I think it's time to get Wash involved. Did he teach you how to do this? This catfish thing?"

"No, I already knew."

Valencia gave her a look that reminded

Megan of Lucy and then led the way upstairs to where Wash was eating at his desk. "We were waiting for you downstairs on the patio. It's a lovely day outside."

Wash didn't look up as he set down his sandwich. "Did Lucy call you about this girl? Sylva Wright? I'm trying—" Valencia's shadow fell over his screen, and he blinked and glanced up as if he hadn't realized he'd been talking to actual people. "Sorry, what?"

"Megan tells me she's been practicing a form of social engineering known as catfishing. Did you know anything about that?"

He frowned. "No. But it's a great idea—" Then he spied Valencia's frown. "Isn't it?"

"She thinks she found Cherish's mother."

"Really? Because she'd dropped off the radar even before Cherish was arrested. If I didn't know better, I'd think she was in witness protection or something. But obviously not, if you found her." He sounded uncertain. "Except—"

"Why didn't anyone else?" Valencia put in. "My thoughts exactly." She gestured for Megan to join Wash. "Megan, can you show Wash? Let him retrace your steps, maybe dig a little deeper."

She left them to work, and Megan pulled up a chair beside Wash. He shifted his keyboard to her, and she signed into the fake profile she'd built up.

"Who's Grant Tyson?"

"No one. Just a guy from soccer camp."

"The one who got you in trouble at the party?"

Was it wrong that the edge in his voice made her smile? As if he were volunteering to be her own private Superman. If he only knew the truth. Her smile faded. "No. That wasn't Grant." She navigated to the page where she'd found a posting by a woman who could be Cherish's mother. Then she stopped. "Wait. Did you say Sylva Wright?"

"Yeah. Your mom just texted me to see what I could find on her. So far all I have is that she sings and plays with a Zydeco band in New Orleans, and right now they're in Asheville, playing at some big busker's festival."

"Because she posted on Cherish's mom's wall. She said she wanted to meet her. They took things to private chat, so I don't know any details." She scrolled down to the post and showed him.

Wash took control of the keyboard once again. "Okay, yeah, not so bad," he muttered, as his fingers typed. Within a minute, a chat transcript flashed up on the screen. "People always forget about the accessibility features." He bounced his wheelchair for emphasis. "They work both ways, you know?"

She had no idea what he was talking about but couldn't help but match his grin. "So this says Sylva is going to meet Cherish's mom tomorrow."

Wash kept typing. "Except..." He gave a low whistle. "Except that is *not* Cherish Walker's mother. Your catfishing caught another catfish. See here? The profile has posts shared dating back some years, but in actuality it was only created a few months ago. And look at these likes and shares—all designed to catch the eye of someone like Cherish. Remedies for burn scars. Henna patterns and designs. Photos from Craven County hiking trails and nature overlooks. Catnip to a homesick kid on the run for a decade."

"So is Sylva really Cherish?"

"No. Her profile is legit—and here's her band's website. See there, the singer? That's Sylva." He pointed to a tall black woman with flowing braids and a wide smile. It wasn't clear exactly who she was smiling at, but she was clearly happy.

"Why does this Sylva want to meet Cherish's mother?"

"More to the point: why is fake Cherish-mom so eager to meet Sylva?"

Chapter 20

By the time they met Lucy at the courthouse later that afternoon, TK and Warren had arrived at a bit of a detente. He would answer her questions, but only exactly as she asked. She tried hard not to take his prickly defensiveness personally. He treated her as if she were a defense attorney grilling him on the witness stand, as if they were opponents. It was exhausting, like trying to pry information out of a oyster guarding its pearl. She was relieved to let Lucy take over as Warren walked them through the scene of Cherish's escape.

Although much smaller than Weirton, Hartfield reminded TK of home—the river winding through the valley; the way the buildings huddled together, built up the side of the mountain, as if seeking shelter; the fact that the most prominent buildings were the churches and the courthouse. Given the evidence of flooding along the riverbanks, it probably wasn't a coincidence that they were also the buildings perched highest along the mountainside. In fact, it seemed that the road literally stopped at the courthouse, or rather at the three-story parking garage beside it. In front of the courthouse the road circled around an oval of grass with three flagpoles at its center. Beyond the courthouse was a park, complete with bandstand and gazebo along with playing fields that stretched out to the forest, creating an abrupt transition from civilization to wilderness. Above the trees, jagged limestone cliffs jutted out from the mountainside.

"Walk me through everything," Lucy asked Warren, as they gathered on the courthouse steps. "She arrived in a detention transport van. What was she wearing?"

He didn't need to refer to his notes.

"Regulation reflective DOC transport jumpsuit. Slip on sneakers. Ankle manacles chained to a belt, hands cuffed in front and also secured to the belt."

"Underneath the jumpsuit?"

Now he hesitated. "It was April. Cold and raining. It's easier to let a prisoner keep their inmate tops and bottoms on for warmth than to try to bundle them into a raincoat."

TK glanced up at that. "Somehow that didn't make it to the official report."

"What's it matter? She took it all with her anyway. That's why it took us so long to get a scent for the dogs—we had to go back and dig her dirty sheets out of the laundry at the detention center. They never were able to get a track."

"Sure they were even Cherish's sheets?" Lucy asked. "If someone at the detention center was helping her—"

"Staff all checked out."

TK noticed he didn't mention the other inmates. She met Lucy's gaze, but Lucy was already moving on. "They took her in from the van through the side door, correct?"

Warren nodded and led the way, using the buzzer to attract a guard's attention. The guard ushered them inside, and Warren continued the tour. "Courtrooms are on the floor above. They would have used this secure elevator."

The guard used his key to call the elevator down and then again on the interior to select the floor. Then he returned to his post as Warren, TK, and Lucy rode up one flight, the elevator creaking and moaning every inch of the way. The doors opened onto a narrow corridor. TK created a floor plan in her mind: they were now on the opposite side of the building from the public entrance. Solid walnut doors lined the corridor—judge's chambers and private entrances to courtrooms.

Warren led them down the hall to the short corridor that led to the public side of the building. "Here's the bathroom she used to change. Her attorney left the clothes for her— after they were searched, of course."

"The attorney, she bought the clothing for Cherish?"

"From Goodwill. White blouse, women's medium; blue blazer; pair of black slacks. Set her back all of a buck fifty."

"Shoes?"

"No reason to bother—not like the jurors would ever see her feet."

"So the full inventory would be socks and underwear, sneakers, khaki top and pants, orange jumpsuit, and a blouse, blazer, and pair of slacks?" Lucy asked.

"And a cotton tee. Why?"

"You didn't find any of it?"

"No. Like I said, she bundled it all up and took it with her."

"No one noticed a girl carrying a bundle that included a bright orange jumpsuit?" TK asked.

He shrugged. "The Staties thought she maybe tossed the bundle out the window and retrieved it afterward."

"Why would she waste time doing that?"

"I thought the window was locked," Lucy added.

TK glanced around the inside of the

bathroom. It held a single stall along with a sink, mirror, paper dispenser, trashcan, and nothing else. She crossed over to the window and tried it. It had no lock; instead, it couldn't open at all, the pane of frosted glass secured by a metal frame to the outer wall.

"It's a new window, different from the one back then," Warren explained. "And yes, the window was locked. Before and after she escaped. She didn't go out that way."

"But she could have thrown something out the window," TK said.

"Maybe," Warren allowed.

TK frowned. "She'd be taking a risk that no one saw—not to mention wasting time to retrieve it. Seems like a lot to chance just to have a spare pair of clothes."

"Not if it slowed down the K9 team," Lucy pointed out. "They were the best bet to track her, and between the rain and the delay and having a questionable scent sample, they were sidelined."

"What does that window open onto?" TK asked, peering through the frosted glass. "Is that the parking garage?"

"Yes. We locked it down immediately. No cars were stolen, and no one left without their vehicle being searched."

Lucy said nothing, just twisted her mouth in a half smile. "TK, do you have the photos from that date?"

TK pulled her tablet out of her messenger bag and scrolled through to find the photos of the bathroom. "Everything looks the same," she told Lucy. "Except the window, of course."

Lucy glanced through them, paused on one, and then nodded. She moved past Warren, ignoring his scowl, to lead the way back out to the corridor. "And the guard was turned this way, back down toward the judges' chambers and the rear hallway?"

"Right. There was a disturbance in Judge Miller's courtroom and it spilled out into the hall. Domestic. The bailiffs were having a hell of a time separating the parties."

"Giving Cherish her chance." Lucy started down the hall in the opposite direction, toward the public area where Cherish would have blended in with her new clothing. Then she stopped and looked back. "If you think Cherish threw the clothing out the window before she left the restroom, then she was already planning her escape. How did she know the guard would be distracted? That the coast would be clear for the few moments she needed, exactly when she needed?"

Warren stopped short, almost tripping over his own feet as he stutter-stepped. He recovered quickly, but not fast enough to hide the look of dismay on his face. "She just got lucky is all," he finally muttered.

"Smarter to be lucky than lucky to be smart," TK said in a low tone that earned her a glare from the SWAT lieutenant. "At least that's what my mom always said."

Lucy said nothing. She kept leading the way, following Cherish's path out of the building, with Warren and TK trailing behind. She stopped inside the main doors in the space before a visitor would reach the metal detectors. "What are these?" She gestured to the large pottery urns that sat along each side of the entrance. "Umbrella stands?"

"They're not allowed inside the courtrooms—potential weapons. If people want to check them at the desk instead, they can, but most everyone just leaves them here—or they don't bring them in at all."

"It was raining that day, right?" Lucy continued out the doors, but this time miming grabbing an umbrella from the stands and opening it just as she crossed the threshold. "That explains why she wasn't caught on the security cameras," she said, glancing up. "An umbrella would have hidden her from the waist up."

"I'll have Wash review the CCTV and pay attention to the shoes," TK said, pulling out her phone. "White slip on sneakers should be fairly obvious, now that he knows to look for them."

"If the camera angles catch the feet," Lucy said. She turned to her right, heading for the parking garage beside the courthouse. "She'd be exposed for what, fifteen, twenty yards at most?" They reached the corner of the garage. The sidewalk continued to the official entrance, but the wall was only waist high. Lucy easily swung a leg over and instantly vanished behind it.

TK and Warren followed. "I told you, we locked this place down right away. The attendant said no cars went in or out at least ten minutes before she ran."

"Cameras?" TK asked.

"She wasn't spotted on any of them." He nodded to ceiling where the security camera sat behind a wire cage. "But it's easy enough to figure out the blind spots."

Lucy ignored him, continuing to cling to the shadows the wall provided until she came to a stop a few feet down. "There's the bathroom window." She pointed up. Because the courthouse was at the top of the hill and the first floor of the garage angled in below ground, the second floor bathroom window would have opened just above the top floor of the three-story garage.

"Too far to jump but maybe close enough to throw something," TK said, judging the angles and distances. "But where could she go from the garage roof? She'd be exposed, with no way out."

"Exactly what I've been telling you," Warren said, as they trudged up the interior stairwell.

They emerged onto the roof. The backside of the garage was dug into the mountain's rock wall.

"See? Nowhere to go. It had to be by car." Warren sounded gleeful, but Lucy's smile only widened.

"You're right. She didn't come this way. There's another possibility." Lucy strode down the steps, and TK and Warren followed her until they were back in front of the courthouse. But instead of stopping, Lucy continued past the building into the park. "No cameras here. No people, either—not in the rain."

"But if she tossed her clothing out the window—" TK said. "That's on the other side of the building. No way could she have retrieved it and gotten over here before the alarm was raised."

"She didn't toss anything out of the

window." Lucy stopped and gestured to TK's tablet. "Look at the trashcan in the picture."

TK frowned. It was a normal white metal trashcan, the kind found in public restrooms across the world. "What am I missing?"

"Not what you're missing; what *it's* missing—"

Then TK got it. "The garbage bag. Black plastic, rain proof."

"And pretty much invisible if she folded it over the jumpsuit and clothing, and carried it as if it were covering a bag or stack of folders."

TK glanced up. The rocky crags above them appeared impossible to navigate. Appeared. But you wouldn't necessarily need to go up over the mountain to escape—you'd just need to follow the tree line above the gorge, along the path of the river, as it led deeper into the wilderness.

"What do you think?" Lucy asked her.

"Difficult. But possible."

"No way," Warren declared, following TK's gaze. "You can't tell me a skinny little girl like Cherish turned her back on a chance for a quick escape via a car and instead went into the mountains with no food, no water, no way to start a fire? Armed with only an umbrella and a few layers of clothing? She'd never have survived—that time of year, it got down to freezing at night. We'd have found her body for sure."

Lucy turned to him with a smile. "And yet, you never have. Because Cherish Walker was not only smarter than you gave her credit for, she was stronger. She knew how to survive, and how to outlast your search parties—that were looking in the wrong direction. All she had to do was wait you out."

TK scanned the steep terrain on the other side of the valley. "The Appalachian Trail runs along there, doesn't it? Crosses the river?"

"The trail's about twenty miles on the other side of the mountain, past some of the most rugged wilderness you can imagine, yeah."

"That was her escape route. Get to the trail. Beg, borrow, or steal clothing and a pack along the way. Hike to a road, hitch a ride—there are vans ferrying hikers to hostels and campgrounds, right? Who wouldn't stop for a tired solo hiker like Cherish?"

"If I were her, I'd stay on the trail all the way to where it ends in Georgia," Lucy said. "Not far from Atlanta."

"From Atlanta she could go anywhere." TK smiled at Warren. "It's easy to be invisible in a city like Atlanta. And by the time she made it there, your searchers would have been long gone, have given up."

"Which means," Lucy added, "that the only question left is: who helped Cherish escape? Because the timing is just too damn perfect. She may have made it out on her own, but someone had to give her the chance to run in the first place."

TK nodded. "We need to find that guard, the one who escorted her and was outside the restroom."

"Gleason. We questioned him, and so did the Staties," Warren said. "He never wavered, and there were no signs of a payoff or any other reason why he'd help Cherish. He even passed a polygraph."

"Was he connected to her family in any way?"

"Not that we could find. And believe me, in small town like this, we would have known."

"Where's he now?" Lucy asked.

"He retired a few years back."

"Can you get me a phone number or address? I'd love to talk with him."

Warren frowned. "I'll see what I can do. But I don't think he's your guy. If Cherish was as quick-thinking and resourceful as you say, then she probably heard the commotion in the hall, figured it was her best chance, and just went for it."

"Maybe. But I'd still like to ask Mr. Gleason his thoughts. He's the closest thing to an eyewitness that we have—not to mention the last person who saw Cherish before she vanished."

CHAPTER 21

SYLVA WAS THE TETHER that kept me sane and grounded those first few months after my gran died. I never even got the chance to talk to Gran, to explain what really happened, to tell her I was sorry for bringing all this down on her. Who knows what she thought of me before she went? No one bothered to tell my caseworker until after she was dead and buried; then he told me, but it was all too late. As if my needing to say goodbye didn't matter—which in this system built not for justice but for the convenience of the courts, it didn't. As a juvenile I had no say in anything, only my "advocate" did, the case worker who always got my name wrong and was constantly running late.

Maybe if my case hadn't been so high profile—at least for our tiny rural community—or if there hadn't been so many appointments, meetings with social workers and counselors and psychologists and other kinds of doctors trying to figure out my "intentions" and "maturity level" and "rehabilitation potential," then I could have done what I always did and quietly faded into the background of the detention center—become invisible enough to grieve in private.

But there was no avoiding the spotlight as I was constantly pulled out of classes or meals or from the commons area to be searched, shackled, and sequestered in the back of the center's van, led to my next interview or hearing. I'd return to another search, extra homework, cold sandwiches instead of hot meals I'd missed, and glares from the others along with the occasional beating if Sylva wasn't around. Although none were as bad as that first—no one wanted to risk Sylva's wrath.

She said they were jealous—any escape

from the monotony of the center's rigid schedule was considered a special treat. She was probably right, but I didn't really care. I just wanted it to all be over with so I could go home to my real life.

Poor, silly, deluded kid lost in a sea of denial. Sylva tried her best to prepare me, to explain what the adults on the outside who now controlled my life were doing. But I didn't listen; I was too numb with grief.

It wasn't until much, much later, when I had the chance to finally watch all the videos and read all the articles, that I realized how massive the tsunami racing toward me had been. No wonder I'd been swamped when it finally hit...and by then I'd lost Sylva, my lifeline. Eight months after I arrived, she turned eighteen. We had cupcakes to celebrate—Nurse Helen brought them in as a special treat. The next morning, Sylva was gone.

And I was alone. Still the youngest at the detention center, but no longer the most innocent.

I think I went a bit crazy. Provoking the

others. Although most of my original tormentors had long since been released, cooped up like that, adolescent emotions running high, it was always easy to find someone willing to hurt me. Poor Nurse Helen—the hours she spent patching me up, talking to me, trying to ease my pain with Bible passages and pathetic bromides.

Then, finally, seeing that nothing could pry me from my self-destructive despair, Helen let me use her phone to call Sylva. For the first time since she'd left, we could talk freely, no worries of recordings or listening ears who could use my words against me later.

She'd made it to New Orleans, just as she'd always dreamed. She was performing with a street band, and had found a cheap room—large enough for two. As always, she had it all planned. I would set up a booth doing henna tattoos for tourists, she'd keep up her singing, and most importantly, we'd be together. Free. Together. Forever.

Magic, intoxicating words.

More tempting than Eve's snake or any forbidden fruit.

A chance to start over. A chance for a new life. A chance to make everything right.

All I had to do was speak my truth.

Juvenile hearings were held in the two-story office building that housed our county Children and Youth Services as well as the Family Court. The only thing that made it different from the building where my dentist had his office was that there was a guard and a metal detector at the front door. Of course, since I was already in shackles, we didn't go through that door; we used the side one and took the back elevator up to the courtroom.

It wasn't court like what you see on TV. The hearing room for Family Court was more like a conference room, with the judge sitting at the head of the table. From the conversation between the lawyers and judge, it sounded like there had been a lot of meetings that they never invited me to. I always felt like I was playing catch up with my own fate. Most of the time they never even asked me to speak—and if I tried to ask a question, the judge would tell me to talk to my lawyer, who was always on his way somewhere else and never had time to answer.

This was also where I met with my probation officer and case manager. They listened to my questions but would tell me they couldn't answer, I needed to ask the judge or my lawyer. It was like being caught in a whirlpool, Ulysses and his crew navigating uncharted waters. I quickly learned it was best just to say nothing, because nothing I said was going to get me home any faster and definitely could and would be used against me.

Until the day a month after I called Sylva, when I had my chance.

"It's the best offer you're going to get," my lawyer—actually, my fourth lawyer, they shuffled around so fast I didn't bother to remember their names since they never bothered to remember mine—told me. This one was a woman. White, like all the others, and all so young that I knew more of the real world than any of them. "Plead guilty, show remorse, and the judge will sentence you as a minor. You'll be moved to a regular prison when you turn eighteen, but released just three years later when you're twenty-one. That's only three years, Cherish."

Funny how her "best offer" math of three years didn't take into account the almost four years of my life I would spend in juvie before I was granted the pleasure of being transferred to a real prison for three more years. How stupid did she think I was?

Seven years before I'd be free to join Sylva. I'd spent less than a year in juvie, and I knew I'd never survive seven more years locked up.

She seemed irritated by my hesitation. "There's a lot at stake here, Cherish. I worked very hard to make this deal happen. I even got the victim and the arresting officer to sign off on it."

"Warren?" I raised my head. Any deal that involved that snake, Warren, had to be poisonous. "He wants me to take the deal? And so does Jack?"

"All you have to do is plead guilty and explain to the judge how sorry you are and that you accept the consequences of your actions. Then, in seven years, you're a free woman."

I pushed her pen aside.

"Cherish, if you refuse this deal, the judge will charge you as an adult. You'll be facing life without possibility of parole. Do you understand that? Spending the rest of your life behind bars? Not juvie; real prison. Forever. Every single day until you die. No chance of getting out."

Tempting. It was all so tempting. Except...it was also a lie.

I was so sick of lying. Of hiding behind silence. Sylva had taught me better—had showed me that being invisible wasn't a strength but a weakness, a temporary escape from my problems. She'd taught me to be strong, to risk, to be vulnerable, that fighting back didn't need to hurt anyone—that the truth could be a powerful weapon.

So many things she'd taught me that I didn't understand until that very moment when I was faced with my own choice. She'd had the courage to live her truth despite the fact that it cost her everything, her freedom, home, and family—she could have lied, hidden behind a story, and her family would have embraced it and welcomed her back home. But she'd refused, choosing to speak out even when no one wanted to hear.

Truth is truth, she'd tell me as we lay together in the dark. *It's the one thing no one can ever take away from you, Cherish. I'd rather be put on trial for telling the truth than sentenced to a life living a lie.*

I was weak, I admit. I actually took the pen up, my hand shaking, ink splattering the virgin white paper...but Sylva's voice filled my mind; her strength, her beauty, her faith in me. No one had ever believed in me like that, not the way Sylva did. More than belief—acceptance. She saw the real me, the one hiding behind the silence and lies.

I hurled the pen across the room with all my might. "No."

Finally, I was ready to tell the truth—but could I trust anyone to listen?

Chapter 22

Lucy drove them to their motel—the closest one was forty-five minutes away in Cleveland—and checked them in while TK went to grab some takeout for dinner. By the time she returned to Lucy's room, Lucy had Wash on video conference and was updating him on their progress. Apparently McCabe had been hounding Wash for news after Lucy had ignored his nine calls and seven texts.

"TK," Wash called out when she moved into his line of sight and began to open up containers brimming over with ribs and barbeque, "I heard you got to visit a slaughterhouse. Sure you're up for ribs?"

Lucy inhaled the savory aroma and could barely resist the urge to dig in and forget about the case.

TK smiled at the camera. "That place definitely gave me the creeps—but not enough to give up my chance at decent ribs and brisket."

"I was just telling Lucy about the progress Megan's made—that girl has a knack, I'm telling you."

"She and Wash found Cherish's roommate from juvie," Lucy explained. "A woman named Sylva Wright. Along with a possible lead on Cherish's mom. Only problem is, they have a meet set for tomorrow morning at a resort in North Carolina on Lake Hiwassee."

"Warren said he'd arrange for me to talk to Gleason, the guard. I can keep hanging with him if you want to check it out," TK said, after she wiped BBQ sauce from her mouth. "I think he's finally starting to warm to me."

"Enough to let you carry your pistol?"

"Enough to maybe let me ride up front with him instead of in the back seat."

"Did you track down anything on Cherish's mom's connection with the Reapers?" Lucy asked Wash. To TK, she said, "The trailer park guy said she took off with the Reapers a few years before Cherish went to jail. He said another Reaper told him she was killed in an armed robbery, buried as a Jane Doe."

"I got nothing," Wash answered. "It's like she vanished—about six months after Cherish's arrest. And when I say vanished, I mean like blank slate."

"Fits with what he said. So maybe she *is* dead."

"Then who's meeting with this Sylva?" TK asked. "Or do you think Cherish has been hiding out with her mom and they'll all be there?" Then she frowned. "No, that makes no sense."

"We think someone faked the mom's social media profiles, and is trying to get Cherish to take the bait," Wash answered.

"To what end?" Lucy asked. "Reapers who think Cherish knows something? Or want her to pay back her mom's debt to them?" She shook her head. Motorcycle clubs had their own rules, and long memories when it came to payback and revenge. "I have a friend still with the Bureau, Jake Carver. He was undercover with the Reapers and helped take them down. I can reach out and see if he knows anything about Cherish's mom; maybe find out who filled the power vacuum in the Reapers once their leaders were convicted."

"These MCs are so well-organized, sometimes the leaders run them from their jail cells," Wash said. "But I don't get what the Reapers would want with Cherish. She was just fourteen—what could she know that would hurt them now?"

"Keep looking," Lucy said. She turned to TK. "Did you find anything else we should be following up on?"

"I wish. Warren and I drove all over this damn county, talked to the detention center workers—the ones still around—and even found one or two kids who were there overlapping Cherish's stay. No one had anything good to say about Cherish. They all said the Kutlers were practically saints, and she'd better not show her face around here, especially after getting away with murder. Their words, not mine. Actually their words were a lot more colorful. But other than shooting the Kutlers, no one actually remembered anything about Cherish—I doubt they'd recognize her if she knocked on their doors and asked to stay for supper. Even her social worker and the psychologist who spent hours evaluating her mental status, the best they could give me were generic memories."

"Let me guess," Lucy put in. "She was quiet, kept out of the way, never said much."

"Exactly. And these were the people paid to advocate for her, who should have been searching for any detail to sway the judge. I know it's been a decade, but no one could be that forgettable."

"Maybe it's just that her crime was so much more memorable?" Wash suggested. "Like that was the legend that everyone talked about, so no one paid much attention to the girl who pulled the trigger because they were focused on the victims?"

"Oh, everyone remembers the victims, believe me," TK replied. "Hank could out-throw, out-run, and given a chance, out-fly Superman before Cherish killed him. And Jack, well, he pretty much walks on water—" She paused. "Funny, though, a few folks mentioned he's had problems. No specifics, just a few sighs and things like *He could've made so much of himself, if only*—that kind of thing."

"McCabe said he was working at his dad's financial firm in Nashville," Lucy said. "So he can't be doing too badly."

"Still," Wash added, "getting shot in the face, losing an eye, probably a bunch of surgeries and rehab and all that, I'm sure it wasn't easy."

They all stared at Lucy. No, at Lucy's ankle. She'd come close to losing it back in January, and was still struggling six months later. Where would she be in a decade? she couldn't help but wonder. Would she still need the brace? Be back using the cane? Maybe things would go badly with all the hardware the surgeons had left behind, and they'd need to amputate after all.

"I'm sure it wasn't," she said. "Let's track him down and set up an interview. In the meantime, we'll focus on the courthouse guard, the Reapers, Sylva Wright, and whoever is pretending to be Cherish's mom."

TK nodded and turned to call Warren to set up the visit with Gleason. Lucy focused on Wash. "You said Megan is the one who found the fake social media profiles?"

He looked away. "Yeah."

"How exactly did she do that? She's grounded from electronics. And knowing how to set up a fake profile? Or did you help her with that?"

"Kids know about catfishing," he said, evading her real questions. "Plus I'm sure you've warned her about it, right?"

His lips tightened, and she knew he wasn't going to betray Megan's confidences. Which meant there *was* something to betray. As soon as she got home... "Okay, thanks, Wash." Then she realized she hadn't heard from Nick. "Nick already picked her up, right?"

"Yeah, they just left."

"Just now?" Nick should have been there hours ago. Of course, the cell reception in Craven County was fickle at best, but she hadn't received any messages. With her luck, they would ping her phone in the middle of the night now that she was in an area with half-decent coverage.

"Yeah, his flight was delayed by the weather. Didn't you hear? That hurricane, Delilah? It's shifted east. It's playing hell with air traffic—it'll be worse tomorrow once it touches land and heads north. You guys should plan on staying put after your morning appointments because it's headed your way."

CHAPTER 23

WHILE LUCY LEFT EARLY the next morning to
drive over the mountain for her meeting with
Sylva Wright, TK remained behind to finish
interviewing the people on their list in Craven
County, starting with former courthouse guard
Lionel Gleason.

She guessed it was a good sign that Craven
County's violent crime rate was so low that their
SWAT lieutenant could spend so much time
playing host to two outsiders, but she had the
definite feeling that there was more to Warren's
generosity in once again volunteering his
services as chauffeur.

"You're keeping tabs on us," she accused

him later that morning, when he picked her up at the motel coffee shop. "Reporting back to the sheriff."

He didn't blink. "Would you like someone poking around in your business in your jurisdiction, getting your folks riled up over things that happened eleven years ago?"

Put that way... "I understand why you're doing it. Just saying you didn't need to keep it a secret."

"Guess I figured it didn't need saying. Thought it was pretty obvious." When they reached his cruiser, he opened the rear door for her and arched an eyebrow when she hesitated. "Still the rules."

Climbing into the rear seat, she sniffed— he'd sprayed it with some kind of air freshener. Didn't mask the stench—rather, it enhanced it in a weird chemical way—but it was the thought that counted.

"Tell me about Gleason," she asked, as they turned onto the two-lane highway, heading east. It was mid-morning, but the sun had only just cleared the peaks before them. Warren flipped open a pair of sunglasses and lowered his visor. "Did you work with him?"

"Technically, the courthouse guards are all sworn deputies, but they're mostly older, looking to finish out their years until they retire. Know what I mean?"

"Wallflowers. They dress like the real thing, cash a paycheck, but spend most of their time propping up a wall."

Warren nodded. "Right. I never knew the guy except to nod to when I was at the courthouse on a case."

TK smiled. At least she was getting more than the yes-no answers he'd treated her to yesterday. Warren was warming up to her—must be her sunny disposition. Next thing you knew, she'd be riding up front, rules or no rules.

"Where's he live now?" They'd reached the turnoff for Hartfield, but Warren kept going straight, the two-lane highway devolving into a narrow, twisting road without a shoulder or a guardrail. And yet, peppered among the craggy ledges and steep, forested slopes, she'd catch glimpses of large houses—the mansions Warren had mentioned yesterday.

"Up the river. He likes to fish."

They turned onto another road that hugged the side of the gorge, following the river. The houses here were small, older cabins and frame-built homes that had high water marks staining the trees surrounding them. Most had docks angled out over the water. No whitewater here; the river was wide enough that it grew calmer, with quiet eddies behind large boulders. Several men in waders were fly-fishing, spaced apart yet clustered together, aiming for the same still water.

Warren slowed the car, peering at the fishermen. "He's not there. Strange. He's usually out on the water at first light."

"He knows we're coming. Maybe he waited."

"Guess we'll see." He steered the car around one final bend, coming to a stop in front of a neatly kept log cabin with a green tin roof. Warren waited a minute before leaving his seat and opening the door for TK in the back.

"Gleason," he called.

TK followed his lead, staying near the car in plain view of the house. But no one came to the door, and no curtains fluttered at the windows. "Maybe he is out fishing," she said. "And we just didn't see him."

Warren said nothing; just motioned for her to stay. He approached the house, one hand on the butt of his gun, and knocked loudly. Then he peered in the windows.

TK moved to the side of the house, ignoring his glare, and headed to the rear. There was a large deck overlooking the water—so close that you could practically fish from it, she thought. Beyond it was a small dock with a flat bottom boat swaying against the pilings it was tied to. Beside the dock, a large weeping willow stretched out over the water, its fronds dancing in the breeze.

And beneath it, face down in the water, arms and legs spread-eagled by the current, was a man.

CHAPTER 24

LUCY SPENT THE DRIVE over the mountains to the resort on Lake Hiwassee rehearsing what she might say to Sylva. She'd downloaded tracks of Sylva's music to listen to on the way, hauntingly lyrical ballads that incorporated Arcadian French, Negro spirituals, and even a hint of Native American harmonies. Sylva's vocals were entrancing, and the toe-tapping Cajun Zydeco styled-songs made even Lucy, forever rhythmically challenged, want to dance. Nick would love them. She made a note to buy a CD or two and have Sylva sign them for her to give to him. Music was the only thing Nick hoarded, refusing to throw away any format: CD or old-style vinyl, even glitchy cassette tapes he'd recorded as a kid.

That might be a good way to break the ice, Lucy thought, as the road wound along beside the lake that appeared on the map as a sinewy Chinese dragon sprawled possessively over the North Carolina side of the mountain range. Finally she pulled up to the gates of the resort, paid five dollars for the privilege of entering the public areas, and arrived at the restaurant overlooking the lake. On the western side of the mountains the clouds had been gathering, whipped up by a fierce wind, but here the sun was shining, reflecting from the water where several small sailboats and kayaks were visible.

Lucy was early, allowing her time to choose a seat on the far end of the terrace where she could pretend to watch the boats while actually watching the entrance and the people inside the restaurant. Old habits, Nick would say—even as he held the door to allow her to enter a public space before him. Not out of gallantry, but because she needed to assess a situation before putting him or Megan at risk. She often wondered how the old-fashioned gesture had come into being—had women been held in such low regard that men had used them as human shields by allowing them to enter a potentially dangerous space first? Nick argued that it was the opposite, that by revealing the presence of innocent noncombatants, men had signaled to each other that a higher code of conduct was now in effect.

Her coffee had just arrived when she spotted a woman striding past the other diners, heading her way. Sylva Wright was only twenty-eight, but she carried herself with the confidence of a much older woman—no, not just older...wiser. An attitude earned through experience, not youthful callousness. Lucy nodded to her and gestured to the seat opposite.

"Ms. Guardino?" They shook hands. "Thanks for coming up. We're playing a wedding this weekend and they're putting us up here. Not that I'm complaining." She leaned back, assessing Lucy. The waitress approached, and Sylva ordered sweet tea while Lucy stuck with her coffee.

"Thanks for meeting me," Lucy said, once the waitress had left. "I know this must be rather awkward—and like I said on the phone, I'm not looking for you to break any confidences."

She paused, waiting for Sylva to fill in the blanks, but the younger woman merely smiled and nodded. Expecting Lucy to show her hand first—exactly how Lucy would have played it herself. Lucy decided to take a gamble and go off script. "I like your music. I know you're based in New Orleans now, but you grew up around here, right? Any native American influences? I thought I heard some of their melodies in your music. Along with Gaelic and Cajun French and African-American."

Sylva nodded, a wistful smile creasing her lips. "My mother's family's part Cherokee, part freed slaves who sheltered with the Nation. My aunts and cousins still live on the res just north of here. My dad's family worked the copper mines and smelted iron—they're Scotch-Irish. When I moved to New Orleans, I fell in love with the Cajun traditions. Guess you could call my music a cultural melting pot."

Lucy noticed how Sylva relaxed while discussing her music. But as Lucy glanced across the lake to the foothills of the Blue Ridge, the mental map in her mind unfurled, another piece of the puzzle that was Cherish Walker falling into place. "When Cherish escaped, she didn't go south, did she? She went north. No one would follow her onto the Cherokee Reservation—given that it's sovereign territory—or have any reason to look for her there. She was safe with your family until you could bring her to New Orleans and start over."

To Sylva's credit, the other woman didn't do more than blink. Lucy was fine with that; she wasn't here to incriminate, she simply wanted Sylva to understand that Lucy was serious about finding Cherish.

"I need you to get a message to Cherish," she continued. "She needs to know that the original charges have been dropped. You can check with Justice for Youth if you don't believe me—or Cherish can."

Clearly Sylva hadn't heard the news. She

frowned, and covered it by taking a sip of her iced tea. "If what you say is true, wouldn't Cherish still be facing charges for escaping custody?"

"Those were dropped as well. But she should know—you should know—that the DA could refile the original homicide charge if they chose."

"So nothing has really changed except there's no more bounty on her head." Her gaze grew distant, and her tone echoed with sorrow. "If she wants to live her life freely, she's as good as walking into their trap. They'll just lock her away again."

"Doesn't she feel caught in a trap now? Ten years living as a fugitive—that has to take its toll."

Sylva eyed Lucy. "You have no idea. Ever know anyone with agoraphobia? Fear so intense that you panic at the thought of stepping past your doorway? Terror at the thought of the wrong person recognizing you? Constantly hiding, skulking in shadows woven by your own lies, afraid you'll stumble and forget which lie you're living today?"

Lucy gave an inward shudder. What Sylva was describing was a lot like what Lucy had gone through after her mother was murdered and she'd injured her leg. Grief combined with PTSD, Nick had diagnosed. It had been like living in a dark cave with no light left in the world, and had kept Lucy a virtual prisoner for months. She couldn't begin to imagine living like that for a decade. "She's lucky she had you. You were her lifeline."

"Sometimes it feels more like an anchor chain. Only we're both at the bottom of the ocean. Drowning."

"That's why you wanted to meet her mother?"

She jerked her chin up. "You know about that?"

"I know Cherish's mother is dead. What I don't know is who you're meeting or what they really want."

There was a long pause. "You could have told me all this over the phone."

"I could have. But would you have believed

me?"

"Why should I believe you now?"

Now it was Lucy's turn to smile ruefully. "Because you're smart. You did your homework. Lord knows, it's easy enough to find me online." One of her greatest regrets was the way the media had turned her private life public. The more sensational the case Lucy broke, the more they seemed to feel the right to own her life...leaving her as trapped, in many ways, as Cherish Walker.

"All right, then. What do you want? Besides hoping that I can somehow get a message to Cherish."

"I'd like to stay. Watch. See who you're meeting with."

"And you're certain it can't be Cherish's mother? She's really dead?"

"We're still working to confirm it, but as best we can tell, yes. She died while Cherish was still in custody."

"So it was all for nothing, then."

Lucy waited.

"You know she's innocent, right?" Sylva

finally continued. "It was self-defense. I don't know the whole story—and she's never told me, so don't even ask. But the one thing I do know is that everything Cherish did, she thought she was protecting the people she loved."

"Her family? But her grandmother died a few weeks later—she could have recanted her testimony, forced a plea bargain." Lucy paused. "Her mother... Somehow she thought she was protecting her mother by confessing?" Cherish's mother had been with the Reapers by then—and from the rumors she and TK had gleaned, the Reapers had been running the drug and prostitution trade in Craven County. Could the Kutlers have been involved as well?

She thought about a quiet young girl, with no adult supervision, no one anyone would even take notice of if she went missing. Cherish had initially said the Kutlers had driven her bike off the road. Youthful stupidity, or something more calculated?

"How well did you know Jack and Hank Kutler?" she asked Sylva.

Sylva recoiled, wrapping both hands

around her glass to anchor her. "Well enough to know they weren't what they pretended to be. Those boys would have given the Devil himself a run for his money."

CHAPTER 25

Watching Sylva meet with the woman named Lucy, I was a nervous wreck. It was the first time in a decade that I'd left the relative anonymity of New Orleans to accompany her and her band to Asheville. So much cooler, she told me, as we slept with our windows open to the mountain breeze. Nice to be near home, she said.

All I could think was, we were *too* close to home. To people who might know me, might remember me. To the Reapers. Maybe to my mother?

That last hope was why I'd finally agreed to come. For eleven years, I'd kept my word; held my silence. Remained hidden, in the dark, afraid every single day that they would find me. Terrified my mom would pay the price.

Those first few years I'd lived life like a haint: sleepless, barely eating for nerves, racked with fear that some day there'd be a knock on the door or footsteps behind me, followed by a gunshot I'd never hear. Seemed like if I were the Reapers, that'd be the easy way out.

Sylva said I was being paranoid, that I didn't mean that much to the Reapers—after all, they'd had plenty of time to cover their tracks from that night, and what could I actually say to hurt them anyway?

After the first few years I realized—and Sylva often reminded me—that the Reapers had no reason to try to track me down except for the bounty still on my head. I'd kept my end of the deal; there was no reason for them to spend the time and energy. If I screwed up, they already had all the leverage they needed to use against me: my mother. Sylva even suggested that my mother wasn't really in any danger—that she'd stayed with the Reapers because that was exactly where she wanted to be.

Those were the nights when we'd argue, and she'd remind me how young I'd been, how easily manipulated. She never understood how delicate the situation was. That me and my mom were just two strands of an intricate web that could fray and break at any time. It was the only thing we ever argued about, and after ten years, I knew it was the only thing that could break us.

I had to choose: Sylva, or a promise a terrified young girl had made on the night she almost died.

Sylva had guessed most of what had happened that night, but not all of it. And I couldn't tell her—every time I tried, the words literally would not pass my lips. There was simply too much at stake, magnified by a decade's worth of worry and fear. She knew the Reapers were involved, and had figured out my mom was at risk. That the Kutler twins and their family weren't the saints everyone thought they were. But of course, I never told her about the person at the center: the Peacekeeper.

Back then, I wasn't even sure myself he

was involved. Not until that morning at the courthouse bathroom when I'd gone inside to change, only to find Deputy Warren waiting for me.

"What the hell were you thinking?" He'd pushed off the rear wall of the tiny room, his words thundering at me almost before I could close the door. "Turning down the plea bargain? Do you have any idea how hard I had to work to make that happen? To get the Reapers and the Kutlers on board?"

I froze, clutching my bundle of new-to-me clothes. Glanced behind me at the door.

"Don't worry about Gleason. He works for the Reapers—the reason he got the assignment of escorting you. I were you, I'd be more worried about the decision you and I are facing now, Cherish." He drew his pistol. "Seems to me, I can end this all right here and now. I'd be a hero, stopping a violent felon from escaping."

I had to swallow twice to find the spit to talk. "I kept my word. I didn't say anything."

"Not yet, you didn't. But it's a whole other ballgame now that you're facing adult time.

You're a kid, Cherish. No way in hell can we trust you to keep silent, not facing hard time, life without parole. Because sure as certain, as soon as Jack Kutler opens his mouth on that witness stand, you're going to be found guilty."

He was right. These past few weeks since I'd turned down the plea deal, all I could think of was what Sylva had told me: better to be put on trial for telling the truth than sentenced to a life living a lie.

If it came down to it, if anyone gave me a chance to tell them everything that happened that night, I would. Not in open court, where the Reapers would hear and then kill my mom, but maybe to a cop I could trust—I'd even considered Warren for the role, silly me. Luckily, I'd realized I could never trust anyone local. But the FBI or the DEA? They could go in and save my mom, arrest the Reapers, and set me free.

In my mind, it all spun out like a TV show or movie, ending with Mom and me together, hugging as explosions filled the sky behind us and the bad guys were handcuffed and led away.

A stupid, childish fantasy—quickly blown away by the reality of Warren and his semiautomatic. "How long have you been working for the Reapers?" I asked.

His cheeks blossomed red, eyebrows colliding as he scowled. "I don't. Everything I do is to protect the people of Craven County. If that means turning a blind eye to some of the Reapers' business dealings—"

"Like with the Kutlers?" I guessed. "They were doing more than dealing drugs and girls, right? They were disposing of bodies back in the slaughterhouse."

"Where better? They had all the tools and privacy you'd need. They've been taking care of bodies for generations—since back in the day of revenue men and carpetbaggers. And would still be at it if not for the twins' stupidity."

"So you know I'm innocent."

"It's more complicated than that. You're lucky I'm around to keep the Reapers honest— otherwise they would have had you killed already. But the deal with you and your mom, that's just one piece of the puzzle. I also had to negotiate a truce with the Kutlers—Jack's being an ass. The only reason he agreed to the plea deal you turned down is he wants to kill you himself, but if anything happens to you and it comes back to him, then the Reapers have no choice but to step in and deal with him. See what I'm saying? It's a delicate balance. For two years, I've protected the folks of Craven County from the Reapers, made sure they kept their violence and most of their dealings far away from here, but now you and the Kutler boys are threatening to upset everything. I'm sworn to protect the peace—but I can't do that if you talk, Cherish."

I wasn't ready to move forward; my mind was still trapped in the memory of that night. "Why did the boys have me there? Why did the Reapers bring my mother there? Was it to kill her? Dispose of her body?"

"No." His voice softened. "Cherish, your ma, she works for the Reapers. You know that, right?"

My nod was intended more to rearrange

my thoughts than to answer him. Stupid me, I thought working for the Reapers meant doing their washing or cleaning up after them. Of course the kids at school knew exactly what my mom really did, but I'd always blocked out their name calling.

"She's a whore." The words felt like a slap as soon as I said them. A blow so hard the rest of the world rocked and swayed. "But that night—did she come to rescue me? With Gran sick, maybe Mom didn't want to risk me going into foster care? So she came...for me?" My voice faltered, my hopes crashing against Warren's granite expression as his gaze hardened.

"She didn't know you were there. The Kutlers, they owe a lot of people money—gambling debts. The boys aren't supposed to get any girls from Craven County, that's the deal. They're meant to recruit them outside the county, not here at home."

"Recruit?" I remembered hearing on the news about a gang in Charlotte—kids younger even than Jack and Hank—forcing their own girlfriends to become prostitutes. Gran had shaken her head, said all the decent men had gone and died in the war, and now my generation was lost.

Warren's gaze shifted away from me to the pistol in his hand. "We don't have much time."

"If you kill me," my voice was a tight thread, unspooling into a thin whisper, "what will happen to my mom?"

"There's no reason for the Reapers to hurt her, as long as you're not a threat." He sighed and lowered his gun. Then he raised his other hand, a set of car keys dangling from his fingers. "There's another option. It's a junker, but it'll get you out of here. Parked down behind the bakery on Walnut."

I stared at his offering, not trusting him. "This is a trick. A way so you can kill me without anyone suspecting. Keeping you and the Reapers out of it."

"I could do that here and now if I really wanted to. Everyone would be happy—except maybe Jack Kutler. I tell you, that boy's got some twisted thinking. No wonder he and Hank were so happy to take over running the slaughterhouse from their old man." Even though I hadn't taken the keys, he holstered his pistol.

"Are you saying I should go to the Reapers? Be with my mom?" I had a fleeting fantasy of me rescuing her. "That way they won't have to worry about me talking." Or they could just kill me themselves. Mom wouldn't let that happen...unless they killed her, too. My mind whirled with possibilities and consequences.

Warren frowned at the idea. "There's no free rides with the Reapers. Everyone earns their keep. And there's only one way for a girl like you to do that." He gestured with the keys. "Take them, Cherish. Leave."

"I should just go?" After all these months of being locked up, other people telling me when to eat and sleep and open a door, I was overwhelmed by the idea of freedom.

"It's your choice. If you keep silent, I can keep the Reapers from coming after you—at least as long as Stone is running the show. For your ma's sake, you'd best pray the feds never catch up to him. If anything happens to him, you and your ma are as good as dead."

"You as well."

He sighed. "Me as well. And a lot of the peace-loving folk here in Craven County. You remember what it was like a few years ago—back even before the Reapers took over your cabin? You were just a little girl, but I'm sure you heard about the shootouts, the killings that came with the drugs."

I nodded. With my dad gone, I'd been scared all the time back then, and those stories had only made things worse. I'd hoped they were just that—stories to scare little girls, keep them awake at night, but obviously they were real.

"It was like the wild west around here. Too many bodies for the morgue to even keep cold. Until Stone and I brokered a deal, a way to restore the peace. It's a fragile thing. But if you can keep your mouth shut, it just might hold. For awhile, at least."

I took the keys. I had no intention of using

them—I still suspected a trap—but it was better than any plan I had. And God help me, once my fingers closed around the freedom those car keys promised, I wasn't thinking of my mom. She'd made her choice. I didn't think of the innocent people of Craven County or even exactly what it would mean—being on the run, staying quiet for the rest of my life. All I could think of was Sylva, waiting for me down in New Orleans.

All I knew was the faint surge of hope that I'd have a life, be free to go where I wanted, be with who I wanted, instead of rotting away behind prison bars.

"Think hard, Cherish. It won't be easy. Can you do it? Can you help me hold the peace? Keep your ma safe?"

"Yes." And my second deal with the devil was sealed. If only I'd had any idea of the price we would all end up paying.

CHAPTER 26

HER DAD HAD WANTED HER to stay home, but
Megan insisted that he drive her to Beacon
Falls. There were too many gaps and holes in
the case. She needed to go back through
everything one last time before presenting her
case to Valencia.

She locked herself in her small office and
tackled the original files, sitting back and
reading—cover to cover—every report. Not
highlighting passages that proved Cherish's guilt
like she had earlier, not trying to built a case
one way or the other. This time she tried to do
what her mother would do: see the whole
picture.

She decided to work backwards, to give herself a fresh slant. First came the judge's ruling dismissing the charges. It was long and boring—she had to borrow a legal dictionary from Valencia—but what it boiled down to was that without Cherish's confessions, there was not enough evidence. Next came the research Justice for Youth had done to build their motion to have Cherish's confession dismissed: medical and psychological expert opinions, case summaries and citations, interview transcripts. Then a lengthy dissertation on the ramifications of the 2012 Supreme Court ruling outlawing juvenile life without parole.

Then she stumbled onto another document, one she'd overlooked the first time through because it had nothing to do with the actual legal case: a private investigator's report from 2010. Submitted by a Cliff Starkey. Good name for a PI. Sounded like a character from one of those old Humphrey Bogart movies Mom and Dad loved.

First she skimmed through the report— easy to do since it was only eight pages long.

Cliff didn't color his facts with any fancy interpretations, trying to pad their impact. She liked that about him. A straight shooter, this Cliff Starkey.

Except...the final conclusion didn't feel like a conclusion at all. It read as if his investigation ended early. She flipped over the final page—Cliff was a paper guy, despite mentioning using some high tech databases in his search for Cherish—but there was nothing there except a notation of final payment received. Weird.

Something else bugged her about Cliff's report. The guy was thorough—he'd interviewed Cherish Walker's case worker, probation officer, two of the detention guards who'd had the most interaction with her, and the courthouse deputy who'd been guarding her when she escaped. He'd also talked to several dozen possible witnesses along her escape route, accessed any surveillance cameras possible, as well as reaching out to homeless shelters and churches within a hundred-mile radius. Each interaction had been meticulously recorded on index cards and then collated and photocopied to create his report.

So what was she missing? She stared at the report wishing she had a window, a view to distract her. No, that would just make her angry that she wasn't outside enjoying the nice weather instead of being trapped in this musty room filled with the detritus that was all that remained of Cherish Walker's old life. She leaned back, closed her eyes, and imagined escaping police custody, going on the run, a fugitive, hiding, scared, no money, no transportation, nothing but the second-hand clothes on her back, headed out into the Tennessee mountains. Cherish had been Megan's age when she'd run off—could Megan have survived?

Probably not. Were they wasting all this time looking for a dead girl? Was that what bothered her about Cliff's report, that he'd been so focused on finding Cherish alive?

She opened her eyes, her gaze on the report's cover sheet with Cliff's logo, contact info, case name, and date. REPORT FOR JH MCCABE, ESQUIRE, REGARDING CHERISH ANNE

Walker, submitted June 8, 2010.

Three years after Cherish's escape. Then she sat up. No, that wasn't what bothered her. It was the date. 2010.

She grabbed the report and banged out of the office, her footsteps thudding on the hardwood floors as she rushed into the conference room where Wash was working. "What year was the Supreme Court ruling making juvenile life without parole unconstitutional?"

"2012," he answered, without looking up from his keyboard.

She sailed the cover sheet over his monitor so it covered his keyboard. "Then why was Mr. McCabe and his Justice for Youth group searching for Cherish in 2010?"

He jerked his chin up at her. "What? Are you sure?" Then he picked up the cover sheet. "The only other data I have from before the SCOTUS finding comes from law enforcement's search for Cherish. Why would a nonprofit be looking for her two years before there was a reason for them to be involved?"

Wasn't that what she'd just said? Grownups, always needing to digest things so slowly—like waiting half an hour before going swimming after eating. But then she realized Wash wasn't processing what she'd told him, he was formulating a plan of action. He handed her the paper, his fingers dancing over his keyboard using a VOIP to dial Cliff Starkey's office number.

"Starkey here." Megan liked that Cliff answered his own phone—and his voice was rough and gravelly, just as she'd imagined it.

"Mr. Starkey, this is George Gamble of the Beacon Group." Wash was short for Washington, his middle name, Megan remembered. "We're reviewing a case you investigated with the possibility of pursuing it further, and we'd appreciate any insights you may have to offer before we decide."

"Which case?"

"Cherish Walker. Back in 2010. She was the girl who—"

"Yeah, I know who she is. So JH McCabe is still on the warpath, looking for her? Good for her, staying clear of that creep."

Megan blinked and glanced at Wash to see if he'd caught that. He leaned into the monitor even though he couldn't see Cliff Starkey since the call was voice only. "Excuse me?"

"Listen. I'm not going to break any confidences here, you understand. But if you're wondering why I dropped the case, it was because I wasn't about to risk my license being an accessory to murder."

"Murder? Mr. McCabe—"

"Isn't Mr. McCabe. I take it you haven't done a full background check on your possible client yet. Let me save you a little trouble. JH stands for John Henry. And McCabe is his stepfather's name. The name on his birth certificate is Kutler."

Megan grabbed Wash's shoulder, her other hand clapping over her mouth before she said anything. "He's Jack Kutler, the surviving twin," Wash said.

"Fooled me at first, too. The plastic surgeons did a helluva job with his face and fake eye, but it's him. When we thought I might have a real lead, something the feds and cops had missed, he offered me half a mil to bring the girl directly to him and then forget all about her—*without* reporting the capture of a wanted fugitive to the authorities. That's when I dug deep and realized what he really wanted with Cherish Walker."

"Revenge."

"Eye for an eye," Cliff said. "Only I reckon that will just be the start. JH McCabe is insane—and I don't use that term lightly. He's been in and out of mental hospitals for the past decade. You'd best steer clear of him."

Wash cleared his throat. "Thanks. We will. But this possible lead—did you find Cherish and warn her?"

"No, sad to say, it didn't pan out. Not that I would have necessarily let her go—there was a twenty-thousand-dollar reward. Although after meeting McCabe, I was starting to have doubts about her guilt. I got busy with other things, had to pay the bills, but I always meant to give her case another try. Guess if McCabe's still looking, she hasn't turned up yet. It might be best to let sleeping dogs lie, though, if you know what I mean."

"I do. Thank you, Mr. Starkey. You've been a tremendous help." Wash hung up and tilted his chair back onto two wheels.

"McCabe made it all up," Megan said. "He never wanted to save Cherish—does Justice for Youth even exist?"

Wash was busy dialing. "Yes. We've done work for them before. They're legit. As is their report on Cherish—her charges were dropped. We verified that before we took the case."

"So he stole their info to get us to find her for him."

He held a hand up as a phone was answered. "Justice for Youth."

"Hello, this is George Gamble from the Beacon Group. I'm trying to reach JH McCabe. I believe he's one of your associates?"

There was a lengthy pause. "No, not an associate, I'm afraid. But he's a donor. Perhaps that's where you saw his name—he's listed on our honor roll."

"Does he volunteer for you at all? Perhaps

by providing legal services?"

"Legal services? Mr. McCabe? No, sir. He's not a lawyer. But maybe he paid for one of our lawyers to take on a case?"

"Oh, of course. My mistake. I'll call his cell directly. Thank you." Wash pushed back from his keyboard, lips pressed together.

Megan pivoted to stand in front of Wash. "We have to call my mom. She has no idea she can't trust McCabe. If he's as crazy as Cliff says, then he might not care about hurting anyone who gets between him and Cherish. She could be walking into a trap."

Chapter 27

Lucy remained at her seat while Sylva moved to the far edge of the terrace, near the café's entrance, to wait for her appointment with the person claiming to be Cherish's mother. Unlike during her talk with Lucy, Sylva now looked nervous, adjusting her seat, glancing into the dining room, then past the terrace entrance to the walkway leading to the parking area. She dropped her napkin once and knocked over the bowl with the sugar packets before stirring one into her tea. Lucy was afraid she would bolt before the meet ever took place, but then a man appeared on the walkway.

Sylva stared at him, looked back into the

dining room, and then rose to meet him. Lucy stood as well. What the hell was JH McCabe doing here? Then she realized: the lawyer must have set up the fake online profile as another means of reaching out to Cherish.

He and Sylva met, McCabe taking her elbow and steering her away from the terrace. Lucy followed. No way in hell was the arrogant attorney going to stiff the Beacon Group, claiming that they'd had nothing to do with finding Sylva—Lucy got here first, and she wasn't about to let McCabe off the hook.

She rounded the corner into the parking lot. There was an Escalade idling in a handicapped spot beside some trees that shaded it both from the sun and from easy view. McCabe appeared at the rear of the vehicle. Sylva was nowhere to be seen. Lucy moved past the other cars blocking her view and approached McCabe from the driver's side.

"Mr. McCabe," she called. "I hope you didn't scare off Ms. Wright. She and I were developing a plan to reach out to Cherish Walker." A white lie, but close enough to the truth to make her point: it was the Beacon Group's work that had solved the case, not McCabe's stupid catfishing scheme.

Then she drew close enough to see into the Escalade's rear compartment. Sylva was there, gasping for air as if in pain, her arms restrained by two-inch wide nylon webbing with a thick ratcheting clasp, the kind used to secure cargo into place on truck beds. McCabe raised a pistol, aiming it at Sylva's face.

"Stay quiet and get in," he ordered Lucy.

A myriad of choices flew through her mind, none of them involving Lucy getting into the SUV. But no matter how fast she imagined herself moving to cross the distance between them and tackling McCabe or drawing her pistol, every scenario gave him more than enough time to pull the trigger and kill Sylva. Instead of moving, she tried to distract him, to pull his attention away from Sylva long enough for her to take action. "Who are you?"

McCabe kept his gaze and aim directed at Sylva. "Get in and I'll tell you everything."

Before Lucy could move, he flicked his free

hand up and out, and a blue blaze of electricity crackled through the air. Not an ordinary stun gun, she realized, as lightning fired along her nerves and every muscle locked into place. A cattle prod. Higher voltage and a shitload more pain.

Muscles frozen, she tumbled to the ground. McCabe pinned her into place with another shock to the small of her back. He slid her shirt up, removed her pistol, tossed her phone, and then threw her into the rear of the SUV. As she drooled, her chest muscles spasming so every breath was a struggle, her vision swimming red, he wrapped her arms and ankles in cargo straps, ratcheting them so tight they bit into her flesh.

"Jack, no," Sylva moaned, from behind Lucy.

Jack...Jack Kutler? Before she could voice her thought, the smell of burning flesh filled the air as he zapped first Sylva and then Lucy. The world grew dim, fading into a blood-red void of pain.

————.————

I FROZE. I'LL NEVER FORGIVE myself for it, but Lord help me, I froze. When I saw Jack Kutler marching up to Sylva, it was like a ghost come back to life.

Sure, his face looked totally different from how I remembered. But the way he moved, that possessive gleam in his eye—at that moment, it was if he owned the world, owned my soul. I shrank back behind the restaurant's pillar, pulled down my hat to hide my face, and said nothing.

When I gathered the courage to glance up again, he was walking Sylva out. The other stranger, Lucy, followed at a distance. It took me a minute to clear my head enough to count out the money to pay my bill. All I could think was: what did Jack want with Sylva? All these years I'd thought she was safe because he and the Reapers knew nothing about her.

Stupid, stupid girl. Ten years was nothing to a guy like Jack. Even as a kid, once he had his mind set on something, nothing could stand in his way. Not an opposition lineman on the football field, not a skinny little girl who'd only wanted to get home out of the storm... The only person who'd ever said no to Jack was Hank...and I'd killed him.

I scrambled out of the restaurant and spotted Lucy beside a large black SUV with tinted windows and an open rear hatch. Was Sylva inside? What had he done to her?

Jack tugged at Lucy's arm. Suddenly he lunged, and she fell. I ran forward, hid behind a parked car, and carefully inched up to look through its windows. Jack was fiddling with something in the rear of the SUV, and then he banged the hatch closed, wiped his hands on his slacks, and strode to the driver's side.

Lucy and Sylva were nowhere to be seen.

I turned and ran. Sylva's Prius was parked near our room. There was a spare key in the wheel well. It had been a long time since I'd driven—I didn't have a license or any form of ID; I was a ghost that way—but it didn't matter. Jack had Sylva. And I was her only hope.

Jack drove ten miles over the speed limit, even on the steep switchbacks, heading west over the mountains. I couldn't take that risk; what if the police stopped me? I didn't care as much about being arrested as I did my mom's safety. The Reapers had the police in their pocket, everyone knew that. Which meant there was no one I could call for help... except maybe the one person who'd helped me before. The Peacekeeper. Or snake, depending on how you looked at it. Warren.

It was a risk. He'd warned me that if I ever returned to Craven County, I'd end up paying with my life. And my mom's. But if it saved Sylva, then it was worth it.

We hit a straightaway where I finally had a few bars on my phone, and I made the call, praying his number hadn't changed over the years. Before me, the mountain peaks were hidden by storm clouds tumbling through the sky, mirroring the black waves of panic that threatened to smother me whole.

"It's Cherish," I said, when Warren finally answered. "Jack took Sylva. I'll do anything you want. Just help her."

He was silent for so long I thought the call had been dropped. Lord knew that happened often enough in Craven, even in good weather.

"Where?" he asked.

I knew the answer to that—had spent the entire drive imagining it, my greatest fears come to life. "The slaughterhouse."

"On my way." He hung up, and I was alone with my fear.

Chapter 28

WHEN LUCY CAME TO, she was lying face down with her chin resting in a small puddle of coffee-smelling vomit. Thankfully, most of it had soaked into the carpet on the floor of the Escalade's cargo area. She was hogtied, unable to straighten her legs enough to try to kick out a taillight or window. She rolled onto her side and saw that Sylva's legs weren't restrained and that she'd managed to prop herself up on the seat back in a kneeling position.

Lucy lay there, forcing air into her lungs, trying to drown out the pain that hammered along her cramped muscles, listening to Sylva and McCabe's—Jack's—conversation.

"She won't come after me, you know," Sylva was saying. "I left Cherish. We had a fight. That's why I'm here in North Carolina. Alone."

"I doubt that, but she'll either come on her own, or I'll have time to have a little fun before sending her a video from your phone. Doesn't matter, either way. She'll still come."

Sylva fell silent, resting her head on the seat, her body swaying as the SUV jostled around a curve. Thunder sounded in the distance and rain drummed against the windows and roof, providing an eerie background noise that echoed through the vehicle.

"You know where we're going—right, Sylva? Can't remember if you ever made it out to one of Hank's parties."

"I never got invited. But yeah, I know where we're going."

Lucy rolled toward Sylva, struggling to contort her body into a position where she could try to loosen Sylva's restraints without Jack seeing her in the rearview mirror. Sylva shifted, stretching her wrists back behind her until

Lucy's fingers could reach them.

"Kutlers have been in the cattle business for over a century," Jack said. "We pride ourselves on taking care of our animals from birth to death—and beyond, if you count slaughtering and rendering. We made use of every part of the cow; nothing left to waste. My great-grandfather made his fortune inventing a hydraulic foot pump that helped skin cattle and freed the operator's hands to wield his knives for the fine work. Then his son created a steam digester, a tank that rendered anything left after butchering into cattle feed. Not a trace left behind. The perfect circle of life." His laughter was tinny, pitched a touch too high.

"I thought your family got out of the cattle business," Sylva said, as Lucy fumbled at the ratchet securing the thick cargo tie. It had some kind of locking mechanism that she couldn't pry loose.

"Yeah. My dad pretty much squandered away the family fortune and sold most of the land. So Hank and me, we got creative. Found new ways to put the slaughterhouse to good use—amazing how profitable it was. Not to mention fun. Hank, he liked to watch, tell me where to cut, when to finish things. Just like how he was with girls. They all found him so irresistible, but nothing would happen unless I was there. It took two of us, one to watch and give the orders, the other to carry them out. But we both had fun. Until Cherish Walker came along. That bitch destroyed my family and ruined my life. I've waited a long, long time to settle the score."

"She lost everything too," Sylva pleaded. "Her family is gone, she's been on the run, never had a life. And you know it wasn't her fault."

"Because of her, I was left all alone!" he thundered. "It was like I was dead inside, alone in the dark. But then when I stopped taking the medication, Hank found me again. He tells me what to do, just like always, and we both have fun. Just like we used to."

Sylva shuddered and looked back down at Lucy. Lucy's fingers had grown numb as she tried every angle she could manage, but the clasp wouldn't budge. Still, she wouldn't give up.

They made a sharp turn onto an even bumpier road, splashing through puddles and bouncing over ruts that tumbled Lucy away from Sylva.

"All this time," Sylva said, her voice a hoarse whisper, "have you been—" She swallowed, unable to finish.

Jack laughed again. "Told you. Me and Hank. We're inseparable. Unstoppable. The dream team—just like back in high school. He tells me how to get the girls, what to say, I bring them home, and then the real fun begins. Took a lot of practice, figuring out exactly what we wanted to do to Cherish—how to make it last, how to make her understand what pain really is. Don't worry." He slowed the SUV to a stop. "You'll see. I promise."

Rain lashed through the car as he opened the door and hopped out. When he opened the hatch, he looked past Lucy, lying helpless, as if she didn't exist. He pushed her aside and reached past her for Sylva. Sylva resisted, but then the damn cattle prod came out and she crumbled. Lightning cracked through the sky, and Jack laughed. He grabbed Sylva and threw her over his shoulder like a sack of feed.

Then he slammed the hatch shut, and Lucy was alone. Even though it was midday, the storm cast the SUV into darkness, the only light the flashes arcing through the sky. She lay there, considering her next step. She was on top of the spare tire and tools, but there was no way to reach them below her, even if she could figure out how to roll the carpet out of her way. There was no inner latch to unlock the cargo door. She thought about kicking off her shoes and sliding her ankle brace off to see if that would give her one ankle enough room to wriggle free, but the straps around her legs were too tight.

Which left going forward. And it was going to hurt, but pain was already cramping her body—better to move now while she still had some feeling left. She rolled up to a kneeling position. Leaning against the seat back, she rocked her body, using the seat as a pivot point.

Every joint felt stretched to near dislocation, but she kept pushing off the floor of the cargo space, heaving her body forward, until finally she was rewarded with enough momentum to go over the seat.

She landed on her face, slipping off the slick leather and bashing into the center console, but once she caught her breath she sat up, her numb fingers fumbling for the door latch. It surprised her when it popped open—she'd half expected Jack to lock the SUV, but he was obviously focused on other things—and she fell backwards.

The ground was soft. Too soft. Water sluiced over her body, tugging her weight into the mud, oozing into every crevice like wet cement. Rain drummed against her face, so fierce she had to close her eyes, and lightning flashed red as thunder rocked the earth around her. Wind blasted the door to the SUV shut—she couldn't return to its shelter now even if she wanted to. As she lay there, soaked to the bone, chilled and trembling, a new sound came: the sound of trees being severed from their roots, tumbling down the mountain side, crashing to the ground.

As if the storm was unleashing Hell, aiming its might at the Kutler slaughterhouse.

CHAPTER 29

THE STORM HOWLED AND SHOOK the Prius. I had the wipers and defroster on high but still could see nothing except silver streams of water and the occasional leaf clinging for mercy against the windshield before it was swept away. But I knew these mountains and this road; I could practically feel my way to the slaughterhouse.

At least, that's what I told myself as the Prius slipped and shuddered its way down the mountain. Then we hit the plateau, and even as I sighed with relief, hoping to pick up speed, the storm hurled its full force at me, slowing the car to a skidding crawl. A tree fell as I passed; thankfully the wind kept its trajectory away from the road, but I felt my stomach go empty, all the air sucked out at the thought of how close it had come to hitting the car. I had to get to Sylva. If it were a mere battle of wills, no storm short of the Apocalypse would stop me.

Finally, I skidded and hydroplaned across the mud as I turned into the slaughterhouse. I stopped behind the black SUV—it appeared empty. My headlights barely pierced the darkness. There were no visible lights on in the slaughterhouse, but then the building had almost no windows. He had to be inside. With Sylva. Suddenly I felt small and helpless. How could I fight Jack? How could I stop him alone?

I scrambled through the glove compartment, searching for a weapon. All I found was a flashlight and a folding knife. They'd have to do. My teeth were chattering— the July heat had been vanquished by the storm—as I shoved the car door open and stepped outside.

Lying in the mud beside the SUV was a woman's body.

"Sylva!" I cried, my words shredded by the

wind. The body moved, struggling upright. Not Sylva; the other woman, Lucy. The one who used to be an FBI agent. She could help me. She'd know how to stop Jack. I ran to her and helped her to sit. She was covered with mud, coughing and sputtering, her hands and legs hogtied behind her.

Leaning her against the SUV, I tried to release the cargo straps restraining her. They wouldn't budge—then I saw why. Jack had threaded locks through the ratchet handles so they couldn't be released. So typical that Jack would have been prepared like this. I flipped the knife open and pressed the blade against Lucy's restraints. "Where's Sylva?"

"Inside with him. Do you have a phone?"

"Help's on the way. Not sure how long, though, not with the storm." I shifted my weight, tugging at her restraints. She winced as they bit tighter into her skin, but it was the only way to get the blade under them. Then I began sawing, our faces side by side, bodies pressed together. "I'm Cherish Walker, by the way."

"Lucy Guardino."

"I know. We did our research before your meeting with Sylva."

"Were you expecting Jack Kutler to show up?"

I sucked in my breath, my vision swamped by the image of Jack grabbing Sylva's arm as if he owned her. "No. We thought it might be a Reaper; someone who knew my mom."

It was Sylva's idea, using her trip to Asheville to reach out to whoever had posted online as my mom. The chance to finally get answers, to know if my mother was safe—I couldn't refuse. But I couldn't let her go alone. Not that my paranoia had done us much good.

"What really happened that night with the Kutlers?" Lucy asked.

So many years keeping my silence. Just like I had when I saw Jack with Sylva, I hesitated. All my fault. So many people dead. Sylva... God, how could I ever forgive myself?

Time to tell the truth. All of it.

"Mostly what you probably already know," I told her, my words stumbling, fumbling, straining, as if I had to shove each one off a cliff to give it life. "The storm. Hank and Jack running me off the road." They'd planned it, planned it all—I hadn't known that then, of course, but later it was oh, so clear. "Taking me to the slaughterhouse. Spiking my drink."

"Did they assault you?"

"No. It didn't get that far." Almost, though. "I was just a kid. The idea that the two hottest, most popular guys in school would even notice me, much less want to be with me—that was almost more intoxicating than the booze. Hank kissed me. Then we danced. It was...nice. Then Jack tried to kiss me, and I pushed him away." I swallowed against a flush of shame. "Then I kissed Hank. By that time I had no clue what I was doing. All I knew was it felt so good. It was like I was a balloon, floating somewhere outside of my body, looking down from heaven."

"The drugs—probably Rohypnol or some variation of MDMA."

The tip of the knife nicked her skin, but I kept sawing. The heavy-duty straps were thicker than I'd realized. I shifted my weight, leaning into her body, trying to increase my leverage.

"Why didn't the police do a tox screen? Or at least a blood alcohol?"

She'd understand once I finished. But right now it was taking all my courage to get through it. "All these years, you're the first and only person I've ever told this to. Not even Sylva. I was terrified what would happen if I said anything. Anyway," I continued, "Jack began to argue with Hank, said he deserved a chance before the others came. I had no idea what they were talking about. I was content just to curl up on Hank's lap and let his hands roam where they wanted. But then Jack threw a full beer can at Hank, daring him. I looked up and he was pointing a gun at us both. I was so scared I almost came back into myself, but Hank just laughed. He helped me to my feet, planted my back to the wall, and told me to hold real still and I wouldn't get hurt. Then he put the beer can on my head."

"He what?" Lucy glanced back over her shoulder at me. I didn't meet her gaze; just focused on my work.

"I guess he and Jack did this all the time. Played William Tell. The whole place was lined with bullet holes. I was so scared I couldn't have run if I tried. All I could do was stand there. The gunshot was so loud I thought I'd never get that sound out of my head. When I opened my eyes, the beer can was still on my head. Jack had missed me entirely. He was swearing, and Hank grabbed the gun from him and said it was his turn. And Jack did it. He stood against the wall beside the door. Hank held me tight against his chest and forced me to hold the gun, his hand wrapped around mine. I was shaking so hard, crying. I didn't want to do it."

"Hank made you shoot Jack."

I could have stopped there, kept the rest of my secrets safe, but Sylva's face floated across my vision, so I kept going. Someone needed to know the truth, and there was a good chance I wouldn't be around after tonight. "No. That's when the door opened and my mother came in, screaming that they couldn't have me, to let me go. Hank swung—he was going to shoot her, but I—I yanked on his arm with all my strength, just as he fired."

"And he hit Jack."

"He hit Jack. When he saw what he had done, he turned the gun on me." Hank's face flashed red, twisted like a demon as it stalked across my vision. "We were against the wall, there was no room to run, so I fought back. I grabbed the gun, twisted and shoved, and both our hands were on it and he slammed me up against the wall, but I'd gotten my finger on the trigger—"

"It was pointed towards Hank?"

"Pointed up, but he was so tall. He was leaning over me, trying to force me down. And it went off. The look in his eyes. I've never seen anyone so surprised. Despite everything, he never expected to die that way. He fell on top of me and we landed on the floor."

"But you said your mom was there? That was real, not a hallucination from the drugs?"

"Very real. I always thought she'd left me after the fire—before that, even, when she let those men, the Reapers, come into our home. I was so stupid. Everything she did, she did to protect me. After my dad died, Gran had her first heart attack, so all our money went to take care of her. But it wasn't enough. So—" I choked. "So a man named Stone came to her. Said there was an easy way she could earn money without even leaving home. All she had to do was let a few friends of his use our house as a meeting place."

"The Reapers ran their drug deals out of your house?"

Lucy was a quick study—she'd filled in the blanks much faster than I ever had, and I'd lived through it all. "It was perfect—we had a cabin in the woods, right on the state line. No way the county sheriff would ever bother them, and they were way too far from any state or federal police. But then..."

"They took over. Began cooking meth there."

"And my mom had no choice but to let them do what they wanted—otherwise they'd hurt me. Of course, I didn't know that. I was so angry, so hateful to her—I thought she was betraying my dad, that she'd turned into an addict or a whore. But then the cabin burned down. I saved her, I pulled her out of the fire, but a few Reapers got hurt and two died. So they said now my mom owed them. Big time. And she had to pay or else."

"They took her. But you and your grandmother were still hostages."

"She had to do anything they told her, or they'd come back for us. I grew up hating her, thinking she'd abandoned me, that she'd betrayed my father and grandmother, wanting to be anyone, anything except like her...and she was giving up her entire life to keep me safe. But..." I couldn't swipe my tears away, not without dropping the knife, all I could do was blink and sniff. "But I guess it doesn't take long for a life like that to wear you down to nothing."

"I still don't understand. Why was she there that night? At the Kutler slaughterhouse?"

"After losing our cabin, the Reapers built another distribution network—this one run by the Kutlers. After all, who would ever suspect the two most popular boys in Craven County?

Plus all their sports meant travel throughout the tri-state area, all under the radar, all to events filled with new customers. Meth wasn't as popular with kids, and the feds were cracking down on it, so the Reapers focused on marijuana and designer drugs that were less risky to produce and even more profitable, thanks to Hank and Jack. They also expanded their prostitution activity—they realized a drug could only be sold once, but a girl could be sold over and over. Hank and Jack helped with that as well, steering girls who no one would miss, who wanted a new life, into the Reapers' hands."

"That's why they targeted you that night?"

"Yes. I was alone and vulnerable. With Gran in the hospital, people might look for me for a day or two, but then I'd be just another runaway lost to the world."

"So your mom was with the Reapers that night, thinking they were picking up a girl?"

"They could've killed her." My voice was stronger now. I was stronger. "I saved her. Just like she'd saved me. I saved her. With my silence."

Lucy waited for me to continue. I'd never dreamed how difficult it would be, saying these things. Putting them into the world, making my worst nightmare real.

It was so much easier keeping the memories locked away, but she needed to know, so I told her how my mother had screamed and screamed and screamed until the lead Reaper, Stone, yelled at his men, "Get her the hell out of here!"

Then he'd stepped inside the office, his eyes seeming to absorb all the light from the overhead bulb as he stared down at me. I couldn't breathe; Hank's body was still on top of me. I thought about playing dead—I was covered in enough blood—but Stone saw everything, including when I blinked.

"What a mess, what a godawful, cockup of a mess." He wasn't yelling, yet his voice boomed through the room, louder than the gunshots. He took another step and the guy with him grabbed his arm, but Stone shook it off. He pulled out his pistol and waved it first at the other Reaper and then at me and Jack and Hank in turn.

"Give me one good reason why I shouldn't put a bullet in all of their heads and make sure the job's done. What a screw-up!"

"Forensics, boss," the other Reaper said. "Three dead kids means the cops tear the whole place apart searching for evidence. Including out back. And we can't be sure how careful the boys have been since they took over from the old man."

My mother's screams finally faded into the distance, and for a second I thought they'd killed her. I opened my mouth to shout for her, but Hank's weight was like an elephant sitting on my chest and it was all I could do to gulp down a whisper of air.

Suddenly my ears are pounding with my heartbeat, and I no longer feel like I'm outside my body. Just the opposite—I feel every single cell preparing to die.

Stone keeps staring right at me. Slowly, careful of where he steps, he crosses over and squats down in front of my face.

"You're right," he tells the other Reaper, who stays by the door. "Get everyone out. Then call our friend at the Sheriff's and tell him he needs to be the first one here, make sure our name stays out of it, and no one looks too carefully in the back. Just a bunch of kids partying too hard. A tragic accident. Then after all the commotion's died down, you'll get the old man and scrub the whole place down. Decontaminate every inch of it. I want you to use so much bleach and shit that you can eat off the floor and still not leave any DNA behind. Got it?"

"The old man will be pretty upset about his boys."

"Do I give a damn? They've been making money off us for years. Give him a bonus, tell him to retire to Florida. This was all his fault anyway, giving the business to the boys so young."

All the while he's talking to the guy behind him but staring at me lying there on the floor. Hank's body is starting to cool on top of me. I'm gasping each breath like it's my last. He cocks his head to one side, then pokes at my face with his pistol. "Now, then. What about you, little girl?"

"Don't you hurt her," I snarl, ignoring his gun. "Don't you hurt my mother."

He laughs and pulls the gun back. The Reaper behind him shuffles uncomfortably. "The boys said they'd roofie her before we got here—she shouldn't remember a thing."

"Oh, she'll remember this," Stone replies. "She'd better, if she doesn't want the whole wide world to come toppling down on top of her." He lowers his face so it's the only thing I can see, filling my vision until all the air I breathe comes from him and stinks of rotting meat and whiskey. "Starting with you being the reason why your dear old ma ends up dead."

I shrink back, but he pins me to the floor with the pistol again, grinding it into the soft flesh below my eye until it hits my cheekbone.

"Don't hurt her," I whisper, each word a gasp of pain.

"I won't. Not if you can keep your mouth shut. That's the deal I'm offering. We were never here tonight. Your ma was never here. The boys never mentioned us, never told you anything about the work they do for us. Especially not what they do in the back. You tell anyone—anyone—about us being here, and I'm going to send you pieces of your ma bit by bit, whittle her down to bare bones, and send you a tape of it all so you can watch her scream and know it was all your fault. Understand, little lady?"

Tears strangle my breath and I think my chest will be crushed as my lungs lose their air, but somehow I manage to nod.

"You keep your mouth shut, say nothing to nobody, and your ma stays safe. You have my word on that. Not a hair on her head will be harmed. But it's all on you. Can you do it? Can you keep your mouth shut?"

I open my mouth to answer but quickly clamp my chattering teeth together and nod again.

"Good girl." He eases up on the pressure against the gun. "So we have a deal? Think hard because this is for the rest of your natural born life we're talking. You can't say anything, not even on the day you die—if you do, your ma, she dies, too. Deal?"

A third time I nod, sealing our fate: my mom's and mine. He stands and returns to the door. "Wait five minutes, then call the police."

Then he was gone. They were all gone, vanished into the night, taking my mother with them.

And now, eleven years later, it was Sylva paying the price for my silence.

CHAPTER 30

AS SOON AS LUCY WAS FREED, she searched the SUV for any weapons, but found nothing except a tire iron. Cherish refused to wait for help to arrive and the cell service was down, so Lucy had no choice but to allow the younger woman to come with her. Together they headed through the quagmire into the slaughterhouse.

Cherish helped by sharing the layout of the slaughterhouse with Lucy. "This ramp leads into a corral where the cows were rinsed off. From there they were herded one by one into the stunning pen. Once they were stunned, the sidewall would give way and they'd tumble into a chute, where they'd be hoisted by a hoof up onto a railing system. Then they'd have their throats slit and be bled out."

Lucy tried to translate the words into a map in her mind. "How do you know all this?"

"Grade school tour before they shut down." Cherish gripped her knife. "The thing to remember is that there are several levels—ramps and scaffolds and ladders connect them—and not everything you step on will be solid. There are trap doors, false floors, and fake walls designed to force the carcass pieces down certain paths."

They'd reached the sliding doors leading inside the large barn. Jack must have brought Sylva this way because they weren't fully closed, shuddering in the wind. Lucy took advantage of the cover provided by the storm to ease the door open a few more inches, enough to glance inside. The small cattle pen was empty, and she couldn't see past the walled chute that was the only way out. "Where do we start?"

Cherish looked past her and shrugged. "Follow the way the cows went."

They edged inside. Rain thundered against

the metal roof, echoing through the confined space.

"There has to be an employee door, right?" Lucy asked, eyeing the chute uneasily. It felt like a trap. "He'll be expecting us to go through the chute."

"You're right. Let me go first—I can distract him, draw him away. Then you follow."

"No way. You're a civilian, I'm not letting you—"

Too late. Cherish dodged past Lucy and sprinted up the incline to the cattle chute. She ducked low, shoved against the bottom of the false wall, and disappeared from sight beneath it. Lucy followed, pushing the wall out just far enough to see into the next space, watching and waiting.

The killing area was as Cherish described: chains hanging from a railing and large hooks dangling free over a shallow vat. A scaffolding about six feet high began on the other end of the vat, allowing men to work both from overhead where they could reach the hoisted hindquarters of the cattle as well as below where their heads would have hung. At least half the lights were out, leaving much of the equipment in shadows, its bulk conjuring images of macabre killing machines.

Cherish had slid down the path, climbing out before reaching the stainless steel vat. Lucy imagined a stunned cow having its rear hoof chained and hooked, being hoisted up high enough for a man to slice its throat over the vat, and dangling in the air as its lifeblood drained.

She couldn't see past the vat, not without pushing the fake wall out further, but she heard Cherish cry out and took the risk. Angling her gaze to her far left, she saw Sylva, hanging from one of the hooks, dangling in mid air by a chain wrapped around her ankle. She was kicking, trying to fight the weight of her entire body pulling against one delicate joint, but it was futile. Lucy grimaced—she knew firsthand how much pain Sylva had to be in.

Then Sylva saw Cherish. "No!" she screamed. "Get out of here. Run, now!"

Cherish released some unseen mechanism and the chain spun out, and Sylva fell to the ground in a heap. Lucy used the noise to cover her movement past the wall and down the chute to where she crouched below the vat, hopefully out of sight of anyone on the other side.

"I knew you'd come." Jack's voice echoed through the space, but Lucy couldn't see where he was—it sounded like he was up high, maybe on the scaffold.

Taking care not to let the tire iron scrape against the steel vat, she crawled along its length until she could see past it. Cherish was cutting Sylva's wrists free, but the chain was still wrapped around her ankle. Movement blurred through the space overhead as a machine whirled and metal clanked. Lucy glanced up and saw that the railing holding the chains was moving—and the slack was quickly being taken up on the chain around Sylva's ankle.

Lucy dashed forward to grab the chain, hurling her body weight onto it to try to keep some slack on it before it ripped Sylva along the butchering assembly line. Cherish made the final cut, releasing Sylva's hands, then she moved to release the hook that secured the chain above Sylva's foot. Sylva was helpless to do anything but lie on the cement floor as the assembly dragged her across it.

Cherish had no choice but to wrench Sylva's ankle, bloody and swollen where the chain bit into the skin, basically using Sylva's own blood as lubricant to allow her to squeeze it past the chain. As soon as Sylva was free, Lucy let go of the chain and it whipped past her, retracting into the railing, following the other hooks and chains clattering down into the belly of the slaughterhouse.

Laughter echoed overhead. Lucy tried to help Sylva to her feet, but it was no good—she couldn't put any weight on her injured ankle. More machinery began to whirl, and crackles of electricity sparked through the dark. The damn cattle prod, Lucy realized. Then she looked down—the floor was covered with water, and all three of them were soaking wet. One touch of that prod could be deadly.

"Which way out?" she asked.

Cherish took Sylva's other arm and pointed

to her left. "That way, through the office."

"That's right, Cherrygirl. Step into my office—remember what fun we had there last time?" Jack's voice seemed to come from every direction at once.

Lucy glanced up through the dim light. He must be watching them with security cameras, using some kind of intercom system tied to his phone, she realized. Which meant he could be anywhere, waiting for them. Still, they had no choice. They half carried, half dragged Sylva to the office door, a solid steel fire door that was locked.

Of course.

"What about back through the chute?" Lucy asked.

Cherish nodded, and they headed back the way they'd came. Jack must have cranked up the speed on the railing system because the chains with their heavy hooks whipped back and forth, almost hitting them as they dove past them. They reached the hinged wall, and Cherish pried it open and held it in place so that Lucy could help Sylva climb up.

Lucy scrambled up after Sylva and pulled Sylva out of the way, but when she turned back to hold the wall open for Cherish to crawl under, the steel wall slammed shut, trapping Cherish on the other side. Lucy tried to push it open once more, but it didn't budge.

Jack's laughter filled the air. "Cherrygirl. It's been too damned long. Let's have some fun."

Chapter 31

AFTER THEY FOUND THE COURTHOUSE guard's body
with his head caved in, whether from a fall
against the rocks on the river's bank or—TK's
bet—some other, more malicious cause, TK
spent the rest of the morning waiting on
Warren. First, they waited for backup from his
department. Then the coroner who called the
State Police's forensic team. She had the feeling
that if it had been just Warren there, they might
not have even have bothered, but she made sure
every investigator arriving at the scene heard
who she was and why they'd come to interview
Gleason. Funny how mentioning Cherish
Walker's name made everyone hustle to pass

the buck up the chain of command.

Which left Warren pissed as hell, sending her back to wait in the car. Although when the storm hit, she was the only one under shelter, so she saw that as a small victory. Until she realized he'd been right—the storm arrived with the ferocious, stunning force of a hammer striking an anvil, washing away any uncollected evidence almost instantly.

Fuming with frustration, she watched as Warren strode out of the cabin and crossed over to the car. After closing the door on her in the back, he jumped into the front seat, phone pressed against his ear. "On my way."

He hung up, frowned at TK through the rearview mirror, and seemed to make up his mind about something. Then he switched the ignition on and wove his way past the other vehicles, turning back onto the narrow mountain road, now covered with mud sluiced down from the mountainside it hugged.

"Where are we going?" she asked.

"Across the valley, up to the Kutlers' place."

"Why? What's happened?"

He was silent for a moment, concentrating on steering as visibility diminished to a small swath lit by the headlights, barely extending out from the vehicle. "Nothing. You said you wanted to meet Jack Kutler. Looks like he's come home, is all."

TK didn't trust his sudden cooperation— Warren had been adamant about their not "bothering" any of the Kutler family. She grabbed her cell and cursed. No reception, not winding through the narrow gorge. She kept it out, though, watching for bars. Finally they climbed out of the gorge and she had one flickering bar. She tried Lucy. No answer; it went to voice mail. "Hey, Warren and I are headed to the Kutlers' farm. Call me when you get this."

She hung up but still clutched her phone, barely registering the violence raging beyond the car. Something didn't feel right. Gleason dying right when they were coming to question him, the one person who'd last seen Cherish Walker before she'd vanished. He'd been questioned multiple times and his story had never changed before—so what had happened now that would force someone to kill him? Because no way in hell did she believe his death was an accident.

Then she spotted a new voicemail left by Wash. It must have been caught in cyberspace while she was out of range and only now had the chance to download. She clicked to listen. "It's me. Lucy isn't picking up. You guys need to know—McCabe isn't who he said he was. Well, he is, but it's not the whole story. McCabe is his stepfather's name. He's really Jack Kutler. I'm not sure where he is right now, so keep an eye out. Call me and let me know you guys are all right. Thanks."

She tried to call him back but kept getting a recorded message that service was temporarily down. Warren's radio crackled with activity: reports of mudslides, flooding, a possible tornado sighting, and finally an instruction for all units to use the radios since the cell tower serving their patrol area was down.

TK pocketed her now-useless phone. If

McCabe was Jack Kutler, then why would Kutler call Warren and invite them out to his house? Maybe he assumed they already knew who he really was? After all, taking your stepfather's name was no crime. But then why not just come out and tell them he had personal reasons to find Cherish Walker? Did Justice for Youth know McCabe was Kutler? Maybe all this was an elaborate plot to use them to get to Cherish.

But what did he want with TK? She was no closer to finding Cherish—Lucy was the one following their best lead. And why call Warren? McCabe could have just have easily called Lucy or TK.

They took a turn too fast, and the wheels spun against the slick mud. Warren slowed down, puddles splashing up on either side of the car as he eased them past downed tree limbs. Then the lane opened up to a clearing, the shadow of the mountain casting them into darkness. There were two other vehicles in front of them: a black SUV and a yellow Prius.

They parked beside the slaughterhouse.

"Wait here," Warren said.

He climbed out of the car, the storm quickly erasing him from view, as TK pounded futilely against the rear door. "Let me out!"

No answer except for the roar of the storm.

CHAPTER 32

JACK TACKLED ME FROM BEHIND and looped a length of chain around my neck. The sheet metal false wall I'd been holding clanged shut. I tried to twist free, grabbing at the chain choking me. No matter how hard I kicked or struggled, Jack merely laughed. He arched me backwards, my feet off the ground, not even able to scream now as he yanked the chain tight, sliding a hook through it to create a noose. It ground into my fingers as I frantically tried to claw it open and find room to breathe.

Then came a clanking noise and I was swinging free, my toes barely scraping the ground, dangling from the hoist. Jack spun me around to face him—I was too short, still wasn't at his eye level, but that didn't stop him from kissing me, my mouth open, gasping for air, his mouth bruising against it. His hands slid along my wet clothing, stroking, grabbing, taking possession. Fury burned away my fear and I stopped struggling.

Now wasn't the time to be afraid, I realized. Now was the time to stall. Give Sylva time to escape. And the best way to keep Jack's focus on me? Fight back.

I bit down on his trespassing tongue. When he jerked back, I flung my head forward, cracking my skull against his nose. He gave a satisfying grunt of pain and I followed up with a knee to his groin—which was a total failure without the leverage of standing on firm ground. The movement sent me spinning as the chain followed the railing.

Jack roared and rushed me as if I were a tackling dummy, propelling both of us deeper into the length of the building. We came to a stop at the next station along the butchering line. He straightened, backed off a step, and then slapped me so hard that I spun like a piñata. I still had both hands clutching the chain at my throat, pinned tight, no way to block his blows as he followed up with a clumsy fake kung fu kick to my side and then a fist to my belly.

How long? was my only thought as I twisted and spun helpless. The pain meant nothing as long as it gave Sylva time. Besides, this was just the pre-game warm up—nothing he did caused any real damage; he was just having fun, a cat playing with the bird whose wings he'd broken.

"Told you I'd show you my beef, Cherrygirl," he said in a singsong, as he pushed me along the track. "Me and Hank, we're going to show you everything we know about butchering. We've perfected our method. I've got my knives sharp, waiting to make you scream."

I debated giving him what I knew he wanted: the hysterical sobbing of a victim. But if I was going to die here, it would be on my terms, not his. I clamped my teeth tight and kept quiet. It only infuriated him more, but that also made him careless as each move he made sent me further along the railing. All I needed was a place where I could plant my feet—then I could work my hands around to the hook digging into the back of my neck, undo it, and free myself.

We were almost to the rear of the building, deep in the shadows since Jack had kept the lights back here turned off. He knew the place well enough to move with confidence, dancing up to the first level of scaffolding to shake my chain from above, threatening to tighten the noose. I had no idea what part of the cow the next butchering station was meant to remove, but whatever it was, there was a trough, maybe six inches high, covered with a metal grate. Exactly what I needed.

Jack vanished into the shadows, singing some weird song, as if calling for his knives. He kept talking as if Hank were here, carrying on both sides of a conversation I couldn't follow even if I'd had the strength to try. Now that my feet were planted, taking my weight off the chain, I was focused on tugging the noose off my head.

Once I was free, I scooted into the space beneath the lowest set of scaffolding, hoping to hide in the shadows until I found a way out. Sylva and Lucy should be long gone—I'd left the keys in the Prius, so the only thing slowing them would be the storm.

Jack returned, doing a strange dance-rap combo that I remembered as his touchdown celebration from all those years ago. He still thought Hank was alive, still thought he was the high school football star, I realized. I held my breath—it hurt to breathe, my neck bruised from the chain—as I crept beneath him. His celebration moves rattled the scaffolding, sending rust and mud down over me. Inching deeper into the shadows, I focused on silence.

Then a bright light stabbed into the space in front of me, blinding as it reflected from a shiny rack of knives. I scooted back but now all of the lights came on, accompanied by Jack's laughter.

"Cherrygal, dumb as a cow," he chanted and I realized he'd herded me here, exactly where he wanted me. He leapt down from the scaffolding, arms spread wide, long knives clutched in both hands. I had nowhere to run, and my back was pressed to the cement block wall. Just like that night all those years ago.

I still had my folding knife. After cutting Lucy and Sylva free, it would be dull as hell, but better than nothing. I slid my hand around my waist to my back pocket, grasping it, carefully opening the blade. Jack faked to one side and then lunged to the other, coming closer and closer with each step. The light filtered through the scaffolding's grated floor, casting warped shadows over his features, making him look like a twisted monster.

He took another step, close enough for me to see that it was no illusion of the light. His eyes had gone wide, his teeth were bared, blood covered the lower half of his face—I'd broken his nose, adding to his macabre appearance— and the light winked from his oh-so-shiny knives.

I drew in a deep breath, to hell with the pain, and braced myself, focusing on exactly where I'd aim: his left groin where there were several major arteries and veins. Anywhere higher and I'd be at a disadvantage with his greater height, plus I'd open myself up to his attack if I aimed high. Low and dirty it was.

One more step, I told myself, watching his hands. Just one more step...

Chapter 33

LUCY HAD NO CHOICE but to leave Cherish behind, despite Sylva's protests. She half carried, half dragged Sylva up the chute and back through the corral to the door leading outside. The rain drove down in sheets, slicing through the air, almost horizontal. Bending over double as the mud threatened to twist Lucy's own bad leg out from under her, they fought through the storm toward the cars.

It wasn't until Sylva nudged her that Lucy looked up and saw a third vehicle parked behind the SUV and the Prius. A sheriff's car! They struggled toward it, and she spotted a figure pounding against the rear window—TK.

Lucy opened the front door—unlocked, thank God—and lowered Sylva onto the driver's seat and clicked the rear door release. TK flew out of the back seat.

"It's Warren," TK shouted over the might of the storm. "He's involved somehow. He was taking me to meet Jack Kutler, and then left me here."

"Kutler's inside with Cherish." Lucy turned to Sylva. "Did he leave the keys?"

She searched and shook her head. "No. Will the radio work without them? We could call for help."

"Phones are down," TK said. "But the radio was working before." When Sylva tried, though, nothing would turn on.

Lucy saw that there was a gun rack adjacent to the passenger seat, but it was empty. "Pop the trunk. There might be more weapons." The trunk opened, and she and TK ransacked its contents. Plenty of ammunition, an AED, and first aid kit that TK handed to Sylva, some riot gear; but no weapons. She did grab two flash-bang grenades and a handful of road flares, sharing them with TK.

She turned to Sylva. "Take the Prius. Go for help."

"No. I'm not leaving Cherish."

"TK and I will help Cherish." They each took one of Sylva's arms and helped her through the mud and rain to the Prius. The car was up to its hubcaps in mud; Lucy hoped it wasn't stuck.

"Don't trust the sheriffs," TK added. Sylva was struggling to position the seat so her damaged leg wouldn't be in the way. "Get the State Police."

"Is there time for that?" she asked, turning the ignition on.

"Just go." Lucy backed away and turned to TK. "We would have heard Warren come in behind us through the side door. Which way did he go?"

"To the front. The office. He has keys." She had to shout to be heard above the wind. Behind them the Prius was slowly turning around, slip-sliding over the mud.

Lucy's bad ankle skidded out from under her, but TK caught her with an arm around her waist. Together they began to hobble toward the front of the slaughterhouse. Before they'd made it halfway across the lot, the ground began to shake, vibrations echoing up to rattle Lucy's bones. The wind shrieked, and the sound of wood striking metal crashed through the air.

They stopped. The lower half of the mountain, where the trees had such a precarious hold on the earth, was sliding down, a tsunami of mud aimed at the slaughterhouse.

———◆———

AS I LUNGED TOWARD JACK, gambling everything on an all-or-nothing attack, the building shook and a strange thudding pounded against the metal roof. Jack whirled, his head hitting the bottom of the scaffolding, and my knife sliced his flank; not exactly the killing blow I'd intended. The noise grew louder, like fireworks going off directly overhead, one booming explosion after another. I took advantage of Jack's distraction to spin away before he could grab me, and I scrambled back down the scaffolding toward the front and the exit.

Suddenly, a blast of wind and rain struck me from behind. The lights flickered, some of them exploding in a burst of sparks, and everything went dark. The roof heaved, a kite tugging at its string, the far end buckling as the thuds became a rush of noise. The entire building shuddered; it felt as if the mountain were coming down on top of us.

I kept floundering through the dark, tripping over grates and vats and equipment as I fled. The roof at the far end caved in, and trees tumbled in through the void, along with a rush of mud that cascaded in like a waterfall. The faint sunlight escaping the storm made it all look so surreal, reflections echoing in every direction. The noise was deafening, and it wasn't until I tripped and fell onto my back that I realized there was water covering the floor, several inches already, rushing and grabbing at anything it could reach.

Throughout it all Jack was screaming and shouting abuse, raging at the storm. He climbed out from under the scaffolding and up to the next level, his arms spread wide as he spewed thunder meeting thunder.

Then came another shriek of sound, this one the sound of metal tearing, ripping itself apart. A segment of the roof split apart, releasing a fresh wave of water and mud directly onto Jack's head, tossing him down from his pulpit. Machinery fell along with the top tier of scaffolding. Lengths of sheet metal flew through the air. The water rose as I huddled beneath the scaffold, metal raining down around me.

Finally the maelstrom eased. The only sounds remaining were the rain battering what was left of the roof and Jack's screams of anguish—worse than any cow being butchered. I eased my way out from under the scaffolding—it had buckled, blocking my path forward—and stood in the weird, dim light, considering my options. I could just make out Jack. He'd crashed down to the floor and was pinned there by debris, barely able to keep his face above the surging water.

It would be easy to kill him. Easy to leave him to die. God help me, those were the first two thoughts that flashed through my exhausted brain. Sylva was safe. Knowing that, Jack had no power over me. But I still had to live with myself—more than that, I had to be worthy of Sylva. And she would never approve leaving a helpless creature to die. Besides, Jack deserved to face the world for his crimes—and I deserved for the truth to finally be heard.

Grabbing a length of metal pipe to use as a lever, I sloshed my way to where Jack lay, his mouth opening and closing like a gasping fish. He'd dropped his knives; one was still nearby, a six inch boning blade, so I took it and slid it into my belt. Just in case.

I crouched down to study the problem, deciding where best to leverage the debris to raise it without causing any more harm. I turned to Jack, who was watching me with silent suspicion. "Don't worry. I'm going to get you out of here."

"I don't think so, Cherish," came a voice from behind me.

I whirled to see Warren holding a shotgun aimed at me.

"Back away," he ordered. He was close, only six feet or so away. No way he could miss at that range.

"No. He'll drown."

"That's the idea."

He must have realized how unbalanced Jack was, must have wanted to cover his tracks—permanently. Which meant I would be the next casualty of the storm. And who would argue otherwise? A brave deputy risks his life to try to rescue a fugitive from justice, only to find that he's too late. Such a tragic tale.

Like hell. The pipe I held was only about four feet long, but if I timed it right and reached far enough... I gave up thinking and calculating and lunged, swinging the pipe like a baseball bat. Warren ducked his head, reflexively twisting his body away, and the shotgun went off, missing me to strike the cement block wall. The pipe hit his elbow so hard he not only dropped the gun, he went down to one knee. He tried to reach for the gun at his belt, but his hand dangled, the arm obviously broken.

He scooted back, his face twisted in pain, and reached across his body with his good hand, trying to get to his gun.

"Stop!" a woman shouted from the shadows behind us. I looked up to see Lucy, along with another woman, this one my age. The second woman darted forward, placing a boot against Warren's chest and holding him down in the mud and muck as she took his gun, handed it to Lucy, and then searched him.

"Cherish, are you all right?"

"Sylva?" I panted, my throat tight with worry. God, it hurt to talk.

"She's fine. Let's get you out of here." Lucy stumbled forward, favoring her left leg as she stepped over debris swirling through the floodwaters. Her partner hauled Warren to his feet and handcuffed his good hand to his belt.

"Jack—" I turned around. Jack had given up the struggle and let his head fall back, his mouth and nose now under water. His face was relaxed and shone white in the shimmering light, one eye shut, the other eye open as if watching me.

I fell to my knees, pushed his head up, and felt for a pulse.

But it was too late. He was gone.

C H A P T E R 3 4

NICK WAS CATCHING UP at his office, leaving Lucy to deal with Megan—who for some reason was even more out of sorts, despite the fact that she'd helped to crack the case. Nick thought maybe it was the fact that Lucy had been in danger, again, but Lucy disagreed. She'd seen Megan worried and anxious. This wasn't that. More like disappointed... as if somehow, Cherish Walker finding a relatively happy ending wasn't the outcome Megan had expected.

They were in the Subaru on the way home from the phone store when Lucy's new cellphone rang. Jake Carver. She took it off speaker and picked up the handset. "Hi, Jake."

"Mom—that's not about my case, is it?" Megan asked. "Why can't I listen?"

Lucy hushed her with a wave of her hand. "Did you hear about what happened?"

"Yeah. Sounds like as usual, you had all the fun while I was sifting through red tape. But I found out what happened to Cherish Walker's mother."

"She really is dead?"

"Yes. But you were right—she was in WitSec. She lived long enough to testify and help bring down the Reapers. Then died of cancer four years ago."

"So all that time, she was keeping quiet to protect Cherish, while Cherish went dark to protect her mother. What a waste."

"I'm not too sure about that. From the notes, when Cherish's mother first came to us, she was a mess. We sent her to drug rehab and got her clean and sober. Her one condition was that everyone stop searching for her daughter and leave her in peace. By then Cherish's trail was cold and no one had the funds to keep looking for a runaway kid, even one accused of murder, so we reached out to the Marshals and came to a mutual understanding about Cherish. For what it's worth, the mom helped put away some pretty bad guys. In fact, she brought down most of the Reapers' drug and sex trafficking. That paved the way for me to infiltrate what was left of the gang once they turned to gunrunning and money laundering. She was a pretty brave woman, if you ask me. Saved herself and her daughter."

Lucy glanced over at Megan. "Can I share this with Cherish?"

"The general details I just gave you, yes. No specifics. You know how it is with WitSec—operational security trumps everything."

"She could have left WitSec and found Cherish on her own." She glanced at Megan. Couldn't imagine leaving her daughter like that.

"My guess is she couldn't risk the Reapers targeting her, and through her, Cherish."

"Exactly what Cherish spent all those years terrified of—doing anything that would threaten her mom's safety."

"You need anything else from me?"

"No," Lucy answered, her tone resigned. "Thanks, Jake." She hung up and turned to Megan. "How about if we swing by and say hi to Grams? The cemetery isn't far."

Megan, still sulking about Lucy not letting her listen into a conversation about *her* case, jerked her chin in a nod. They drove on in silence. Lucy couldn't stop thinking about how silence had doomed Cherish and her mother.

Finally, she couldn't take it any more. "Ready to tell me the truth about the party?"

———

MEGAN STARED OUT THE WINDOW. "I guess. It was stupid. There's no need to make a big deal out of it." Except there was. And Megan felt it every time she looked at herself in the mirror. "I kinda faked my way into that party."

"You mean you and Emma weren't really invited?"

"No, we were—well, Emma was. But it was *how* she got invited." She blew her breath out.

It was all so humiliating. "You wouldn't understand."

"Try me." Lucy grew quiet. She didn't press or try to guess; just waited. Totally not like her.

Finally the silence was too much to bear. "I did it. I wanted to know if Dylan liked me, so I wouldn't embarrass myself if I let him know I liked him. So I pretended to be one of the other guys on the team, and got in on one of their group chats, and they were talking about the party and the girls they wanted to hook up with there."

Lucy straightened, but she still said nothing. Giving Megan room. Room to wriggle like a worm on a hook, Megan thought, as she hugged her knees to her chest and looked anywhere except at Lucy. "I wasn't on the list, in case you're wondering. They laughed when I even put my name out there, said I was—" She faltered. Not a one of them had said anything nice about her, and these were guys she'd played soccer with for years, ever since they'd moved here to Pittsburgh. "Know what they call me? The Stick. Because not only do I look like a skinny stick with no boobs or butt, but because I act like I have a stick up my ass. All because of you. Like I'm some kind of goody-two-shoes whose mommy the famous FBI agent won't let out of her sight."

"Megan—" Lucy started, but Megan knew exactly what she'd say, and she just couldn't bear her mother's sympathy, not now when she was trying to confess.

"No. Don't tell me you're sorry or explain that I'm beautiful on the inside or tell me that this is just a phase and that teenage boys are idiots. That's not the point. I know all that already."

"Then what is the point?" Lucy asked, in a gentle tone.

Megan filled her lungs as if preparing for a deep dive. It felt like something alive pressing against her ribcage, trying to escape. "The point is, I hurt Emma."

"Emma?"

"I was angry. Humiliated. I don't even know why I threw her name out there, and said she was looking to hook up at the party. The other guys jumped all over the idea, added her to the invite list, and even talked about how they were going to get her drunk, maybe drug her..." She paused, waiting for Lucy, but the car was silent except for Megan's breathing, coming fast as she choked back tears. "And I tagged along, let it all happen—I should have never talked her into going, should have told her, stopped it..."

"You did. In the end." Lucy's words came slowly—not absolving Megan's guilt, but acknowledging the rest of the story. They came to a stop at an intersection. Instead of turning toward the cemetery, Lucy drove in the other direction.

"Where are we going?"

"I think before we go see Grams, you need to see someone else. Make amends. It's not me who needs to hear the truth."

Megan pushed her hands against the dashboard as if she could stop the car. "This is the way to Emma's house."

"It's okay. I'll be right there with you."

"I can't—don't make me, please. I can't tell her the truth. She'll never talk to me again. No one will."

"I won't make you do anything. But I think maybe you know deep down inside that you want to do this. Get the truth out there—on your terms. Because you can't keep living a lie, Megan."

Just like Cherish Walker couldn't. Or Jack Kutler. How many people had been hurt by their lies? Pretending to be someone they weren't. Megan had only done it for a night, a few random texts, and it had been exhausting.

Her mom was right. She couldn't live this way, not with this lie festering inside her like a cancer. They pulled up in front of Emma's house. Lucy started to undo her seatbelt, but Megan stopped her. "No. This is my mess. I'll fix it. By myself."

"You sure?"

No. Not at all. Megan had to make a fist and release it once, twice, before her hand was steady enough to open the door. "I'm sure. But you'll be here, right?"

Lucy reached across and pulled Megan close, kissing her on the head like when Megan was a baby. For once, Megan didn't pull away. "Of course. I'm not going anywhere."

Megan climbed out of the car. As she leaned down to close the door, Lucy said, "I'm proud of you, Megan."

"So I'm not grounded?"

"Oh, you're still grounded. I know you know exactly how wrong you were and what could have happened. Not just to you but to your friend. But that doesn't mean I'm any less proud of you. It takes a lot to step up and take responsibility for your mistakes, try to make things right." Lucy surprised Megan by rubbing a knuckle over her eye as if she were tearing up. No way. Lucy never cried—at least not in front of Megan. It would make her all too human, like a normal mom. "Don't worry. Everything will be all right. And I'll be here waiting."

Megan closed the door and turned to face Emma's house. She could do this. She would do this. It would feel awful and horrible and she might lose a friend... She thought of all the terrible things Lucy had had to face—not just the danger, but things like seeing dead kids or telling their families or admitting that a killer had gotten away with murder.

For the first time, she understood why Lucy threw so much of herself into her job. It wasn't because she cared more about those kids she was trying to protect than she did about Megan, it was because it was the only way she could get up in the morning and face the world. Knowing that she was doing the right thing, doing what she could to make the world a safe place for kids like Megan.

It was because Lucy wanted so much more for Megan. And she was willing to fight for it with everything she had. Even if it meant risking her own life.

No way in hell was Megan going to let her down.

Megan reached the front door and rang the bell. "Is Emma home? I need to talk to her. It's important."

———◆———

IT TOOK ALL MY COURAGE to step into Sylva's hospital room. In fact, I'd waited so long in the hall, listening to her parents and the rest of her family fuss over her, that the flowers I'd bought in the gift shop were already wilting. The sales clerk had made me buy two bunches to get enough of the good ones. I'd had to unwrap them to get rid of all the stupid carnations dyed ridiculous cheerful colors. Sylva hated carnations; she called them the Wonder Bread of flowers. But I'd wanted to get it just right—or maybe I was just being a coward, stalling for time.

Finally, it wasn't up to me. A nurse's aide came down the hall with a thermometer and blood pressure machine and gestured to me to push the door open. I held the door for her and stood there as she bustled with importance, checking Sylva's vitals while everyone else was checking me out.

I'd met Sylva's aunt and one of her cousins

ten years ago when I hid out with them at their trailer in Cherokee, but they weren't here to ease my introduction to the remainder of the clan. It seemed like the rest of the known universe was here, though. The redheads with the freckles belonged to the Wrights, and the mixed heritage African-American-Cherokees were from Sylva's mom's side. I guessed that the man perched on the chair scooted up beside her bed was her dad, and the woman nestled beside her on the bed, her hand-painted caftan flowing out like a river of color against the white sheets, had to be her mother.

Sylva saw me and her face tightened around the thermometer in her mouth. Was she trying not to laugh? Or furious that I dared show my face ever again? I held my breath, waiting for the answer, ignoring everyone else who also watched and waited.

Finally the nurse left, with a wry glance over her shoulder in anticipation of the drama about to unfold. I stepped forward with my meager offering. "I threw away all the carnations."

Sylva examined my bouquet with the intensity of a surgeon dissecting a brain tumor. "So you did."

She took the flowers and waited. My empty hands filled with sweat. I rubbed them against the hem of my tank top. "You were right. About coming here. About not living a lie."

A hint of a smile tickled her lips, and I felt bold enough to continue. "Mr. and Mrs. Wright, I'm Cherish Walker. I'm the reason why your daughter has stayed away for so long and the reason why she's hurt now, and I'm very sorry for everything. I hope you'll forgive me."

Sylva nodded, a silent urge for me to continue. It was already one of the longest speeches in front of one of the largest audiences I'd stood before in a decade, but I knew what she wanted to hear. Joy bubbled up through me, squelching my anxiety as I realized how desperate I was to say the words.

"I hope you'll forgive me," I repeated, reaching my hand to take Sylva's, "because I love your daughter very much and she saved my life."

Sylva wove her fingers around mine, forging an unbreakable chain. Her mother glanced at her father, but there were tears in her eyes. I was scared I'd just ruined everything. I couldn't take Sylva away from so many people who loved her, not again.

But then Mr. Wright stood and wrapped an arm around my shoulders, leaning across the bed to gather his wife and Sylva into the embrace. "Welcome to the family, Cherish. And thank you for bringing our daughter home safe and sound."